A BALCONY
over the FAKIHANI

A BALCONY
over the FAKIHANI

Three Novellas by
Liyana Badr

translated from the Arabic by
Peter Clark with Christopher Tingley

introduction by Barbara Harlow

INTERLINK BOOKS

An imprint of Interlink Publishing Group, Inc.

NEW YORK

First published in English 1993 by

INTERLINK BOOKS

An imprint of Interlink Publishing Group, Inc.

99 Seventh Avenue

Brooklyn, New York 11215

Library of Congress Cataloging-in-Publication Data

Badr, Liyānah.

[Shurfah 'alá al-Fākihānī. English]

A balcony over the Fakihani / three novellas by Liyana Badr;
translated from the Arabic by Peter Clark with Christopher Tingley;
introduction by Barbara Harlow.

    p.   cm. — (Emerging voices)

    Contents: A land of rock and thyme — A balcony over the Fakihani
— The canary and the sea.

    ISBN 1–56656–104–3 — ISBN 1–56656–107–8 (pbk.)

    1. Palestinian Arabs—Fiction. 2. Palestine—Exiles—Fiction.
3. Jewish-Arab relations—Fiction. I. Badr, Liyānah. Arḍ min
ḥajar wa-za' tar. English. 1993. II. Badr, Liyānah. Kanārī wa-al
-baḥr. English. 1993. III. Title. IV. Series.

PJ7816.A335S55   1993

892'.736—dc20   92–23387

                                                  CIP

Cover painting by Samia Zaru, courtesy of The Royal Society
of Fine Art, Jordan National Gallery of Fine Art, Amman, Jordan.

Printed and bound in the United States of America

10 9 8 7 6 5 4 3 2 1

A BALCONY
over the FAKIHANI

This translation was prepared by PROTA, Project of Translation from Arabic Literature, founded and directed by Salma Khadra Jayyusi.

Other PROTA titles in print:

The Secret Life of Saeed, the Ill-Fated Pessoptimist, a novel by Emile Habiby. Trans. by S. K. Jayyusi and Trevor LeGassick. 1982; 2nd ed. 1985.

Wild Thorns, a novel by Sahar Khalifeh. Trans. by Trevor LeGassick and Elizabeth Fernea. 1985 and 1989.

Songs of Life, poetry by Abu 'l-Qasim al-Shabbi. Trans. by Lena Jayyusi and Naomi Shihab Nye. 1985.

War in the Land of Egypt, a novel by Yusuf al-Qa'id. Trans. by Olive Kenny and Christopher Tingley. 1986.

Modern Arabic Poetry: An Anthology. 1988 and 1991.

The Literature of Modern Arabia: *An Anthology*. 1987 and 1991.

All That's Left to You, a novella and collection of short stories by Ghassan Kanafani. Trans. by May Jayyusi and Jeremy Reed. 1990.

A Mountainous Journey, an autobiography by Fadwa Tuqan. Trans. by Olive Kenny. 1990.

The Sheltered Quarter, a novel by Hamza Bogary. Trans. by Olive Kenny and Jeremy Reed. 1991.

The Fan of Swords, poetry by Muhammad al-Maghut. Trans. by May Jayyusi and Naomi Shihab Nye. 1991.

Prairies of Fever, a novel by Ibrahim Nasrallah. Trans. by May Jayyusi and Jeremy Reed. 1992.

Legacy of Muslim Spain. Essays on Islamic Civilization in the Iberian Peninsula. Ed. Salma Khadra Jayyusi. 1992.

Anthology of Modern Palestinian Literature. 1992.

Acknowledgements

I should like to thank the author, Liyana Badr, for her kindness and cooperation. PROTA is proud to offer this powerful account of contemporary events as they affect ordinary people and visit their lives with tragedy and loss.

To the translators I owe many thanks. Peter Clark's first translation was done with great enthusiasm. To achieve the most faithful rendition of some of the dialogue which was originally written in Palestinian dialect, Dr. Clark consulted one of Palestine's most ardent scholars, Dr. Ibrahim Muhawi, to whom I owe deep gratitude. It is PROTA's tradition to have all translated texts stylized by a native English speaker, and my thanks go to Christopher Tingley, whose stylizing work, done with his usual impassioned love of literature, completed an already excellent work.

To Barbara Harlow I owe many thanks for readily accepting to write her insightful introduction to this work.

Salma Khadra Jayyusi

Contents

Introduction

Throughout the summer and into the fall of 1992, flights to and from Beirut were heavily booked. Although many of the "balconies over the Fakihani," as in other neighborhoods, have yet to be rebuilt, Beirutis—Lebanese, Palestinian and others—could be seen returning to visit Lebanon's war-ravaged capital with a new vision of possibility. For a decade and a half Beirut had been the conflicted scene of persistently renewed social and political violence. The civil war of 1975–76 had redivided the Lebanese population into Christians against Muslims and further isolated the Palestinians who have lived there as refugees since the creation of the state of Israel in 1948. Six years later, in June 1982, Israel invaded Lebanon and laid a summer-long siege to the city of Beirut that culminated in the departure of the PLO and the massacres in the Palestinian refugee camps of Sabra and Shatila. The ensuing decade, then, saw renewed civil war, the "war of the camps," Syrian occupation, and protracted internecine struggle as multiple and multiplying militias did daily battle with themselves and each other for control over an ever more divided terrain. Now, the fighting seemingly over, a visit to Beirut, even a return, although no longer to the past, has become perhaps imaginable.

It is Beirut, the city of civil war and foreign invasion, however, that is the setting for *A Balcony Over the Fakihani*, Liyana Badr's collection of novellas first published in Arabic in 1983. From Yusra's exodus in "A Land of Rock and Thyme" with her family and the other camp residents from Tal al-Zaatar in the summer of 1975, Su'ad's peregrinations from dwelling to dwelling and Umar's sojourn in the clinic abroad, to Abu Husain al-Shuwaiki's departure "on the last boat of fighters" at the end of "The Canary and the Sea" for Tunis with the PLO in 1982, the collection's three narratives disruptively recount the extremes and exigencies, the displacements, the quotidian struggle, and the threatened existence of the Palestinians living then—and still—in Lebanon.

Badr's stories are written in fragments, the shards of historical destruction, the remnants retrieved from repeated dislocations, and reconstituted in the intimacy of the voices of personal perspectives. "A Land of Rock and Thyme" is Yusra's story, the story of a young girl who was carrying water from one of the few tanks in the Christian-besieged Palestinian refugee camp of Tal al-Zaatar when her father was killed in the shelling of the populated site. When the story opens, she is carrying Ahmad's child, and visiting his grave in the Martyrs' Cemetery. Ahmad, her

husband from the West Bank, the lost "land of rock and
thyme," who had studied radiography in India, and who,
as part of the Palestinian resistance, was killed in an
Israeli air raid on southern Lebanon, carries the memories of Palestine that maintain the link between homeland
and exile, between the *zaatar* or thyme, of the occupied
hills and that other hill in Beirut: Tal al-Zaatar. Su'ad,
then, from a balcony overlooking al-Fakihani, remembers
September in Amman, Black September. Since she had
left Amman for Beirut to marry Umar, the Tunisian who
had come to join the Palestinian resistance fighters, Su'ad
had lived in refugee camps in Beirut and Damascus,
before rediscovering the capital from the balcony over the
Fakihani. Umar, her husband, who survives treatment
abroad for an "unknown germ," is killed on that same
balcony when Israeli bombs destroy the building in the
summer of 1982. Janan too, their friend, remembers
September in Amman as she searches out and collects the
detritus of lives that remain from the shattered building
and its violence-scarred neighborhood. Umar, the martyr, who would be buried at home in Tunis, will be joined
there in "The Canary and the Sea," by Abu Husain, from
Shuwaika, "a village that lies north of Tulkarm." Like
Ahmad, Abu Husain remembers too well the land of rock
and thyme, only to have to revisit it as an Israeli prisoner
of war, captured in the assault on Beirut, transported to
Tel Aviv, and eventually exchanged for an Israeli pilot
and the bodies of Israelis held by the resistance. He is
returned to Beirut in time only to join the Palestinian
fighters as they leave for their own Tunisian exile.

Yusra, Ahmad, Su'ad, Umar, Janan, Abu Husain: three
women, three men, six cross-referenced perspectives

overlooking the city that was Beirut and the Palestinian lives that traversed it, intersected and interrupted by the events and dates that identify the historical narrative and frame of civil war and invasion that themselves inexorably oversee the balcony above al-Fakihani. Their respective stories struggle together against that necessity and its impositions. Like Yusra's search in the Museum, when she had been separated from her mother and family during their brutal departure from Tal al-Zaatar, or Su'ad and Janan's quest for Umar following the bombing raid on al-Fakihani, Liyana Badr's stories here tell of losing families in and to the violence of war. As part of the aftermath of that war, however, and in their very decomposition, the narratives textually delineate the still urgent possibilities for reconstructing relations, for rebuilding the "balconies over the Fakihani," a new, if retrospective, vantage point on the past and future of Beirut.

When Terry Anderson, the "last of the United States hostages" held in Beirut, was released in December 1991, United States media pundits and United Nations mediators alike announced the "closing of a chapter" in Lebanese history. In turn, the many fragments, of history and voice, the scattering of perspectives, that go to make up *A Balcony Over the Fakihani* can perhaps be reread now as the prescient piecing together of the outline of a radically new chapter for Beirut—as heavily-booked flights, from Europe and the Arab world, continue to land and take off at Beirut's international airport.

Barbara Harlow
University of Texas
Austin

A Land of
Rock and Thyme

For hands of rock and thyme
This song . . .
　　　(Mahmoud Darwish, "Ahmad Zaatar")

I　The Picture

I dreamt tonight we were walking together. He always comes to me in my dreams. We were both walking along the road near the Martyrs' Cemetery, but I'd no sooner seen him than he went off. He leapt up, began to move among the graves, then ripped his picture from one of them. I don't know where he went then. I looked round at the graves with their white headstones and the garlands of withered flowers on them. The fresh green grass of spring was all around. I looked for him but didn't know where he'd gone.

My mind's full of the picture, and I was impatient for the photographer to finish it. I'd intended to go and put it on his grave in the Martyrs' Cemetery. But the situation was tense; fighting had broken out again. Who, these days, would dare go to the Martyrs' Cemetery? I had a long argument with my sister Jamila, who finally took the large size picture from me and locked it away in the cupboard. I was pregnant, she reminded me, the baby was due at the end of the month and it would be difficult to run if there was sudden shelling. What should I do then? Wait? My whole life had been spent waiting and waiting—but I hadn't expected to marry a man who'd love me and want me, wait with me, then leave for ever and never come back.

They used to call him "the Indian" in the Damour camp. When I first saw his swarthy features and black eyes, I thought he really was an Indian. When we first talked about it I asked him, "Are you Indian?" and he laughed and laughed, till he almost fell over. "Indian?" he said: "Me? I'm from the village of Jamaain near Nablus, Yusra." It amused him afterwards to remind me that I'd been misled by the nickname and thought he really was Indian.

II Damour*

After we'd left al-Zaatar we lived for about a year at Damour. Our house was at the side of the road, an eerie house with no doors, no windows, no floor and no sanitation—a big house, burned inside like the rest of

---

* Damour was mainly inhabited by Christians, and when it was shelled its inhabitants fled eastwards to the Christian area. Ironically it was the Tal al-Zaatar survivors fleeing from the east who took refuge there.

those in Damour. Stripped of its tiles, the floor was just sand and gravel. The first thing we did was clean it, which took about a week. Mother whitened it with lime, but it was only half white because of the grime and smut. We brought in empty gun boxes that my brother made a door from, and we put up plastic sheets for windows. At night the winds came straight into us because we were close to the sea, and Mother would sit up all night, too frightened to sleep as the wind beat against the flimsy sheets with a sound like shelling. Always she was anxious and frightened, frightened in the winter and frightened in the summer. Mother was the only one who was frightened.

When the Israelis started their airstrike, Mother's nerves were already shattered and we just couldn't stay in Damour. Life there was utterly dreadful. The houses were a long way from one another, whereas we'd been used to having lots of neighbors around us; the shops were a long way off too, and the vegetable market even further away. There was no running water in the house. In time we managed to attach an electric cable to the street light and fix a lamp to it inside the house. But Mother was still frightened. We didn't like Damour and we finally moved to Beirut, into an apartment left empty by its owners who'd fled the fighting.

III   Water Has a Memory

During the final raid on the Tal al-Zaatar camp I was at the water tap, which was in the last part of the camp they attacked and captured from us. Each day, throughout the siege, Jamila and I would take the lower path that led to al-Dakwana. Usually we couldn't even get two jerrycans

5

of water. The water was cut off early in the morning and came on again in the afternoon or the evening. We used to wait eight or ten hours for our turn at the tap. Sometimes our turn came and sometimes an attack started, with shells falling on us like rain. Then the water would be cut off and no one would get any.

In the beginning, at the start of the siege, we used to fill our cans from Jinin School, near the George Matta metalwork factory, sleeping in the broad cellar of which the factory was part. The place was filled with over seven hundred people, who shared it with bits of metal and huge pieces of machinery. We'd lay our bedding out amongst piles of rods and various pieces of machinery used for cutting, smelting and casting, just able to find a place among the chairs, beds and metal cradles that were stacked one on top of the other. Our blankets would be laid on the floor and our belongings put out to the side. We couldn't sleep because of the pungent smell of the metal which got into our nostrils and choked us.

We stayed at George Matta's for about a month. It was a dangerous spot because it was near the Monastery of the Good Shepherd. Every day the women swept the workshop floor and sprinkled water on it, and they'd bake bread on a metal sheet on a kerosene stove. People would knead dough, make bread, go to sleep and get up again in this shelter. In the first days we were sometimes able to go out and fill sandbags to strengthen the defenses of the camp. Even Mother, a month after giving birth, went with the women to fill sacks. Everyone did their best.

From time to time some *fida'iyin** would pass by the

---

* *Fida'iyin*: The general meaning of *fida'i* is "one ready to sacrifice his life for his country." The plural is *fida'iyin*.

6

shelter, reassuring us and keeping our morale high. "Don't be afraid," they'd say. "There's no danger." In the last ten days of the month their visits stopped. None of us any longer had the courage to stick our heads out of the door of the shelter.

The enemy was right on us, and anyone who peeped out would be instantly shot at by snipers. They got very close to us. Only one street now separated us from them; we were at one end and they were at the other. Five people were killed by snipers, although, in the first period of our refuge there, no one was wounded except once, when a shell fell near the door of the shelter and injured several people.

One day a girl popped her head out of the door and saw them sneaking up on the shelter. We didn't hear a sound, but we knew their next attack would be directed at us. We knew the Fascists had entered the shelter next to George Matta's factory and killed a hundred and twenty people, including seventeen from the Shuqair family alone. As the snipers seized the front entrance, our people opened an exit in the back wall, and so got safely away.

We left at five o'clock with only the clothes we were wearing; everything else was left behind. The next day, before the Phalangists could complete their occupation of the district, I went back to the shelter with a group of others to get whatever supplies we could carry. I had to get a tin of milk for my baby brother because Mother's breasts had run dry and she couldn't feed him any longer.

Many people were injured as we left, shot down as though they'd been standing right in front of the rifle. As the snipers fired, the dead dropped one after the other. Those who got out in one piece were the lucky ones.

7

IV   In the Middle of al-Zaatar

After the assault on the Good Shepherd Monastery district we moved to the middle of the camp; there was no space left in any of the shelters, where people were already packed one on top of the other. At the side of the main road, we found an amusement room with pinball tables, called "Flippers," and we reinforced the entrance with lentil sacks and sand, and settled down in the place. It was opposite the Red Crescent clinic, which had now been turned into a hospital and was used for preparing the food there. Flippers had only one, normal-sized room, in which the machines had been placed on one side, and we shared it with those and the clinic's cook. People who saw us used to ask how we could possibly install ourselves opposite al-Dikwana, in such an exposed position. But what else could we do? Mother would answer: "God is our refuge." The simple truth is that there was nowhere else to go. The lentil sacks weren't much help as reinforcement; shells from the 500 mm cannons simply passed over them. Once a shell came and hit the inside wall, and shattered all over the place, one splinter sinking itself into the stomach of my eleven-year-old brother Ali. It buried itself under the skin and black salve was no use for getting it out. Mother tried to take him down to the Red Cross, so that he could be evacuated to the western area with the wounded, but she wasn't able to.

Here, in the middle of the camp, Jamila and I would go each day to fetch water—two jerrycans, which was barely enough for so many of us—there was Mother, Father, three girls and six boys (five after the fall of al-Zaatar).

Living as we did across from the emergency clinic, we'd sometimes have patients coming to us for a drink and at times, too, the cook would take some of our water. Sometimes a hundred people used to gather at the water tap, at other times rather fewer, depending on circumstances. The tap was in a narrow alley, flanked by houses that were all empty, for the area was constantly exposed to snipers. We'd put our jerrycans down in a long row, then hide in the rooms nearby. When the water came on, usually some time after two or three in the afternoon, there'd be chaos as people rushed towards it; nobody kept their place in the queue. One day when I went with Jamila, the day Father was killed, the water came on at two o'clock. There were people, and there was water. We went to it as soon as it came on, but Jamila left, saying she wanted to be home by six in the evening. A neighbor standing near me asked after my father. I didn't know anything. "He's fine," I said, and I laughed because the man lived next door to us and I was surprised to hear him asking after Father when he saw him every day. Half an hour later Jamila came back, her eyes red and swollen.

"What's the matter, Jamila?" I asked.

"Mother hit me," she said, "because I wouldn't come back here and fetch water." Jamila knew that Father had been injured, but thought the wound was a minor one. We were still waiting for our turn around midnight, and it didn't finally come till three in the morning. It was beginning to get light and we were still at the tap. The neighbor came back. "Still here?" he said. "I think you'd better go home."

He didn't want to tell me what had happened. "By God," I said, "I'll stay till I've filled my jerrycan if I die

9

doing it! We don't have a drop at home." I cried that night, I cried a lot. It was chaos. Anybody with a weapon would fill up before us; it made me feel bitterly angry. But finally, at about three, we managed to fill up two jerrycans and leave. At home I found Mother sitting up with my grandmother, which was unusual.

"What's the matter?" I said. "Why are you still up?"

"We're sitting up," they said.

I gazed straight in front of me. Then I looked around. "Where's Father?" I asked.

"He's been wounded in the foot, dear," said Grandmother.

"No!" I said. "I want to see him, now!"

"Go to sleep," she said.

I insisted on seeing him. "Where is he?" I asked. "Has he been hit?"

Jamila put her jerrycan down and fell asleep at once.

"Didn't Jamila know what had happened? What is it? What's happened?"

Jamila heard nothing, she'd fallen asleep from exhaustion. I received the shocking news: Father had been wounded soon after we left and had lived on for another four hours. He saw everybody else, but when they asked him: "Shall we send for Yusra?" he said, "let her get the water for her brothers and sisters." That's what really hurt me. If only I'd been able to see him, to talk to him—one word—while he was still alive. He spent four hours talking normally with them. He'd been wounded by a bullet from a machine gun and had bled internally. There was no first aid available; all the medicines had run out, and there was just salt solution to disinfect the wound. This had no effect.

Mother was at his side and he talked till he died, his wound bleeding. He died at about eight in the evening.

Death had become familiar: there was nobody in al-Zaatar who didn't anticipate their own. There were two taps where we filled up with water. Once, when I was standing there, I suddenly became aware of a man next to me, crying out: "Aah! Aah!" I looked at him and saw that he'd rolled over on the ground and died. Shells often bounced into the middle of groups of people, and the only ones who survived were those protected by fate. All you ever saw was people carrying other people. Our home being by the emergency hospital, we saw most of the wounded. Everyone expected death; no one in Tal al-Zaatar thought to live out their natural life. When Father died the condolence people offered was the heartfelt wish that we ourselves should survive. Nobody knew what would happen any more. You'd be standing next to someone—and an hour later, you'd hear he was dead! There was one young man, I remember, who said: "When I die, put me in this coffin." They made coffins from cupboard doors and there was a door ready. "I'll measure it against my body," the young man said. A moment later a splinter of shrapnel struck him in the back and killed him on the spot. So they did put him in the coffin he'd measured himself for. I'm amazed I've never been injured myself.

It was like a dream. You'd talk to someone and an hour or two later you'd hear they were dead. Nada, a friend of mine, was killed by a sniper, and she was a volunteer nurse. Death reached even her.

I remember Father. He worked on a building site at first, but he was hit in the eye several times when chipping

11

stone, and in the end he was so badly injured he couldn't work any more. In the last part of his life he started up a shop inside our house, selling small articles.

I remember Father. Once when we were in the middle of the camp people discovered a water tank in one of the houses. We had a heavy metal barrel that held one and a half jerrycans, and I would always take that with me to make sure the trip would be worthwhile. But on the way back I felt as if my heart had stopped beating from exhaustion. A metal barrel! When there was an explosion I'd run and run, yet feel I was staying in the same place. Then I'd go on walking with the barrel still on my head. It didn't matter how violent the explosions were—I'd hide behind a wall or in a doorway, but it never fell off my head and there was never a single drop spilt.

But too many people discovered the water tank and they emptied it of water. I went there after that with my brother Jamal, who was killed later, and we were there for about half an hour, scooping up what was left of the water till we could fill the barrel and half the jerrycan Jamal had brought.

Then, almost as soon as we'd filled up, the shelling started. Young *fida'iyin* rushed round us and I felt as though my feet were walking backwards. When we were almost home I simply felt myself being thrown to the ground; I'd fallen over and the barrel of water had fallen with me. I started crying. What else could I do? The tears I wept were not from pain but from frustration. I scooped the water up with my hand, but when I got home there wasn't a drop in the barrel. I remember Father said: "What's the matter? Have you been hit?"

"No," I said.

12

"Are you hurt," he asked.

I said that I wasn't, weeping over the lost water. My knee was bruised and my body ached, but I was weeping out of frustration for the lost water.

V   The Exodus

When we left the camp they said we'd be surrendering. People set out together. Some at night, some in the daytime. Some people left on the Qalaa road and some on the Dikwana road. We were on the Dikwana road, and what a terrifying experience it was!

We set out in the daytime, quite early, at about eleven in the morning. The *fida'iyin* went into hiding, then withdrew from the camp at night, but when we set out, we no longer knew what was happening in the camp and those who stayed behind didn't know what was going on outside. One of our neighbors was sitting in her house when the Phalangists burst in; she thought they were *fida'iyin*. "Up and out of here!" they shouted. She shouted back: "I'm not going! Where can I go?" They killed her together with her son and her husband. Her daughter fled and told people what had happened. Her son—what a waste of life—was fourteen years old.

At first nothing happened on the road we took. Then, in groups, we passed through their posts where they stood on the two sides of the road, and they started killing people left and right. We didn't look at them; if you looked at them and met the eye of one of them, perhaps you might be dragged away. I never looked. They'd come among us and pick out whoever they wanted, then simply kill him. On both sides of the road there were landrovers

13

and armed men with crosses on their necks.

A man was walking next to me, his shoulder brushing mine. They grabbed him by the shoulder. "For God's sake," he said to them. "Which God?" they replied. Before I know what was happening, he'd fallen to the ground; there was a revolver and a single shot to the temple.

We set out in a crowd, with everyone mixed up; a mother didn't even know where her own child was. I seized the hands of some of my brothers and sisters and Mother grabbed the hands of the others. Only Jamal was cheerful. "Load up!" he said light-heartedly, as we got ready to leave the camp. "Load up! We've got to take everything with us. Don't let's leave anything behind!"

He longed for the sea. Why did he long for it? He loved the sea passionately. He couldn't wait to reach the western district. We had an aunt who lived by the sea in al-Awzaai, and he used to go swimming when he was there. He couldn't believe his luck, because he'd be going there, going to the sea. When would we be starting? Before we set off we all warned one another how, if you're questioned, you must answer: "I'm Lebanese." But he was a young man in the first flush of manhood, in his fifteenth year. People had become weak with hunger during the siege, but his face had grown round and healthy. He'd got taller during the siege and his body had shot up in a quite uncanny way. On the way one of them stopped him and asked, "Lebanese or Palestinian?" "Palestinian," Jamal answered. A bullet to the head, just like that.

We passed by him—he'd gone on ahead of us because he was impatient. I just glanced at him, receiving such a shock my feet could no longer move forward or hold up my body. My nerves shattered, but I couldn't stop or lean over him and touch him with my hand. If any of us were to stop by somebody who'd been killed, they'd pick us out and finish us off at once. I couldn't. We moved on, right past him.

I looked at him, stretched out there on his back, as if he was asleep or had fainted. There was no blood at all. Then because they . . . So I *didn't* bend over him. I *didn't* stop. I *didn't* touch him with my hand.

My mother wasn't with me at that moment. When she saw him she fell into the ditch, with my baby brother that she was carrying, in an indescribable state. She was a mother, the mother of Jamal who lay stretched out on the road as if asleep or in a faint. She couldn't stop by him either.

We went on, everyone totally stunned. I don't have any clear memory of it. Death hovered over us all. No one could look to left or right. I can't remember it clearly.

They started picking out the young men who were with us and rounding them up. There were some cars and people who came to get money rather than kill. Mother found a car, paid the driver 400 pounds and the family was crammed in. She didn't know how or where she was going, and we lost our old grandmother who was left behind. "Go and find her," said Mother.

My brother Nimr was with her in the car. He was a young man of eighteen, but they didn't notice him. He'd been with the *fida'iyin* who'd tried to leave the camp by the mountain road the night before. They hadn't been able to break through, and he'd left with many other young men, by the Dikwana road. He hid himself in the crowd, and so got away. While I was looking for my

15

grandmother, the car moved off; I came out of the crowd, but couldn't find it. I found my grandmother. "That's it," I thought, "Mother's dead and so are my brothers and sisters. There's no way out. Everyone's going to be killed." I was terrified.

Suddenly I noticed a man in army uniform, one of the *Ahrar** or Phalangists, I don't know which. He was the one my Mother had haggled with about hiring the car. I went up to him and somehow summoned up courage. "You're the one who fixed up the car for my mother and brothers and sisters," I said. "Find one for me and my grandmother too." I don't know how I managed it, but I talked to him. "Let's have some money," he said. I didn't have any on me, but Grandmother had fifty pounds and we gave him that. "Get up on this truck," he said. It was a garbage truck. "I can't get up on that," I said. "Why, isn't it good enough for you?" he asked sarcastically. Then he came back and arranged a car for us, and I got in with Grandmother. Then a woman came with her family, looked inside the car and saw us. "Do I have to pay for you?" she said. She wouldn't believe we'd paid, and said she wanted us to pay the same amount she had. The soldier got into the car with us and took us along the Jisr al-Basha road as far as the Samaan Gallery, where there were some orchards. "Get off," he ordered, and as we did so some men came by. "Where are you taking them?" they asked him. "Take them away quickly, or they'll kill them and throw their bodies in the orchards." We got back in the car and were taken to the Museum area.

There were people all crowded round, and we new-

---

* *Al-Ahrar* is a Lebanese fascist faction.

comers joined those who'd already arrived and stuck to them. We couldn't have got away from them in any case, because we were united by sound, or rather by sounds— the sounds of weeping, wailing, shouting, sobbing and beating of cheeks and breasts. Everything round us was normal: cars, people, ordinary gas stations, whereas we'd supposed that doomsday had come. It was as if we'd been reborn, but where had our minds gone? Nobody knew. Life was extraordinarily normal around us—so normal it made you crazy.

I rushed madly into the Museum, looking for Mother. I searched among the people there. "Have you seen my mother?" I asked everywhere. I said to Grandmother: "That's it. My mother and brothers and sisters must be dead." My hands beat helplessly against my cheeks, and I wept, no longer knowing anything, except that the Phalangists were detaining people and settling old scores as they chose. Then: murder.

The final slaughter happened in the Museum. I looked and saw a room with a broad display window; it was packed with young men imprisoned inside.

There were a number of killing stations on the way, the last of these, apart from the final one, being the barracks near the Hotel Dieu. Only those destined for long life left there alive!

I saw a woman dressed in deepest black, more than forty years old. She was hitting a man over the head with a piece of wood with a nail on the end of it, and a young man, perhaps a relative of hers, came up and helped her. She was taking her revenge on us. I heard another woman, who was carrying a pistol, say: "I want to pick out the handsomest young men and kill them."

It was summer, and most of the separatists were in their sleeveless undervests. It was hot, really hot. They wore crosses and had black bands tied to their foreheads.

The Phalangist who got us through—or he was one of the *Ahrar* perhaps—said to us: "You chose Jumblat. We had nothing against you till you joined the international left."*

"Grandmother," I said, "I can't live for a minute without Mother and my brothers and sisters. I can't live by myself, can I?" "Be patient, darling," she said. "You're sure to find her."

But nobody had seen her. Mother wasn't there.

Someone, I don't know how, got us to the truck. The Arab Deterrent Force was around us, Saudis and Sudanese. "Thank God you're safe," they were saying. I cursed them in my mind. "God damn you," I thought. "They kill people right under your noses, and you just stand there as if nothing's happened!" The truck belonged to the resistance and it took us to West Beirut.

In West Beirut, I found her. We met. She wept; I wept; but we met.

She'd been told, she said, that we'd been killed in al-Dikwana after she left and that flesh had spattered the walls in the Hotel School where we'd been separated. During her trip her car had been constantly stopped by young men who'd come forward and demanded money, so that the few pounds she had left had disappeared.

And my little brother needed hospital treatment! At the hospital it was difficult to prick his hand with the serum needle because his veins had shrunk from hunger; he was

* Jumblat: Walid Jumblat, leader of the Druze in Lebanon, was the Palestinians' main ally just before and during the Lebanese civil war.

only six days old when we went into the shelter, and the milk had dried up in Mother's breasts because she couldn't get any nourishment. She'd boil lentils for him, then grind them, mix them with water and get him to drink it. When he went on crying and crying, we'd rock him in our arms so that he wouldn't miss Mother's breast. In the shelter I'd lift him up and walk up and down with him, and one of the young men in the camp thought I was married because the baby spent so many hours in my arms.

Everybody left hungry and weak, and many children died. There was nothing to eat except lentils, chick peas and a few cans. Cigarettes ran out and it was a real hero who could get hold of a full packet of them. Some of the young men would wrap *mulukhiya** leaves or tea-leaves in newspaper and smoke that.

Even Father, who had a few cartons of cigarettes in the shop, craved tobacco and longed for a cigarette as he lay dying.

I remember . . . No.

He was forty-six when he died and he had some kind of premonition of it. I once heard him say to Mother: "My time's coming. I'm going to die."

"Of course you're not!" said Mother hotly. "I'll die before you do!"

He told her he'd die as his father had, and at the same age; and so it happened, according to his premonition. My grandfather had been killed by a stray bullet during the exodus from Palestine in 1948. He was forty-six years old.

* *Mulukhiya*: A vegetable with large green leaves which are chopped and cooked with meat or chicken. It is a popular dish in Palestine, Lebanon and Syria, as well as in Egypt.

VI Ahmad

They learned, finally, that Ahmad hadn't been on the plane that blew up in mid-air on its way from Bombay to Beirut. At the glass doors of Kuwait City airport was a middle-aged mother wearing on her head a white cotton scarf embroidered on the fringes with tiny flowers and dressed in a long, black village gown. Her hand was against her cheek and her muscles trembled with fear and apprehension, presaging the arthritis to come.

She wanted to scream, but was quite unable to. Ahmad had just graduated, and his family was waiting behind the barrier in the arrival lounge but neither he nor his plane appeared. Five years abroad and a diploma specializing in radiography. When they heard the news of the crash and Ahmad wasn't there, they thought . . . But Ahmad had enlisted as a volunteer and gone direct to Beirut, to the Damour camp.

"Five years of India! I won't say five years of crushing loneliness and being away from home because I was a member of the resistance and the Students' Union. But I was convinced all that had no kind of value while I was abroad. Did you know that, Yusra? I felt isolated, apart from the world. It was as if I was on one of the peaks of the great Himalayas. I was ill for a long time, and once I fell off a motorbike and was badly bruised. Ill, with just a few Arab friends, in a small village in the middle of India, hundreds of miles from the capital. India? What a place! Indian films are one thing, but the country's another!"

They'd called him "the Indian" at the camp, and one day I asked him: "Are you Indian?" He'd laughed and laughed at my question, which he hadn't thought of

20

before. "Oh no! . . . Would you believe it? Is it possible? Oh no!" He just didn't know how he'd managed to complete five years there. And I'd asked him, "What? Is it true you're Indian?"

"Yusra, do you know what it means to be away from home, there, in a remote part of the world? It's a very real feeling. As real as I am now. Diaries. Look here, at the top of this page:

"December 18, 1975. Today some friends and I were wandering round the market place and one of us went to buy a box of matches. It turned out to be a surprise and a joke at the same time. The box was sealed, but when I opened it I found all the matches had been used. That just sums up India."

I pointed to one of the pages and asked him about an expression written in English. He read it out to me. It was from Tolstoy's *War and Peace* and it said that the factor establishing an army's morale is hard to quantify scientifically, because it isn't related either to the number of soldiers or to any other obvious cause.

On another page I saw curving lines that he'd clearly drawn himself. It was a miniature map of Palestine. I read what he'd written by it: "Remember. This must be turned into a reality." I found nothing else of any interest in the diary: just appointments noted here and there, names scattered about, accounts of monthly expenditure and records of money received, remittances sent through the post.

Ahmad told me about himself. His father was dead, he said, and his mother was remarried in Kuwait to a Palestinian who worked as a van-driver, carrying goods during the day and people who were too poor to afford a taxi at night. Often, as he sat in front of me, he'd become distracted, his thoughts wandering to the West Bank, to his town. He told me about his childhood days and about his married sister Aisha, who was still there and who he hadn't seen since the day he left the West Bank. He thought about her constantly and kept coming back to her. He went on talking to me about her, about the country and about the spring flowers there.

"You're lucky!" I said. "At least you've seen the town you came from."

A town of olives and almonds—that's how I imagined it. He had a tree there, he said.

"What kind of tree?"

"Almond or mulberry, I can't remember exactly."

They had a house on the top of a hill. "We want to build one or two more rooms," he said. "For the two of us. There's an orchard here." He'd draw a plan of his town as he spoke, sketching it out on paper or dust or sand. He hoped to go back; and kept on telling me the 1980s would see us return. He was pretty sure this would happen.

Ahmad was transferred from the camp to work in the administration of the medical department. Then he requested a military training course outside. We'd become engaged before he left, and our letters thereafter were full of love. Before he left I gave him three Fairuz tapes; Ahmad loved Marcel Khalifa and Fairuz, but I've sealed his tapes with red wax now.

The engagement was to last fifteen months; he was a fighter in the resistance and we didn't have much money for extras. We'd planned to marry in the first month of 1981, but he decided, finally, that this should be brought

22

forward; he told his mother and his family to come, and they arrived in October, before I'd had time to get myself ready. We drew up the marriage contracts, and I prepared some clothes. His stepfather and his mother, who wanted to take him back, begged him to leave Lebanon, but he wouldn't agree. I couldn't find a house, and they said they'd only return after our wedding. His mother wanted to take pictures for her family in Kuwait, so they'd know her son was now married.

The house. It was simple, he said; there were no problems about it. A week before we got married I told him I wanted to see the house, and off we went. "God preserve us!" I said. "Is that a house?" It was an abandoned house, isolated amid open country, near an army camp which was one of the centers of the resistance in the South. Around it, as far as the eye could see, were orchards, agricultural land, banana and orange plantations; an empty stone house with no furniture. I was confused and tense. "Is this the house you've been telling me about for the past year?" I asked in astonishment. But I went back, cleaned it and put it in some kind of order inside. "It's all right," I told him. "There's no problem."

We got married there and lived in the house for about ten days. Then his family left, and I went back to my mother's house in Beirut because my leave from work was over.

I stayed with my family for three months and at last found a vacant room we could have moved into—two days after his death. I was a new bride in my parents' home; an embarrassing situation to say the least.

He usually came on Saturdays, because he knew that Sunday was my day off, and the last time he came he gave me part of his salary for the first of the month. I was cold and wearing his field-jacket. I put my hand in the pocket and found some cash. "Is that all that's left from your salary?" I asked him. He tried to conceal things, then explained. There'd been an error in the accounts for the sales of the organization's monthly magazine, and he'd paid the difference out of his salary. There was only three hundred pounds left. I tried to show him this didn't worry me. "There's no problem," I told him. We went out to the movies.

Finally, one Thursday, two days before he was due home on the Saturday, he was killed in an Israeli air raid, from a wound to the head. I'd heard about the raid on Damour and Sidon that same day, but I'd thrust the possibility aside, banished the nightmare from my mind. I didn't think he'd die, that he could possibly die; it never occurred to me even once. The Israelis' surprise raid got him when he was in the camp near Sidon.

This happened during the day on Thursday, January 29, 1981.

In the first month of the year.

At two o'clock in the afternoon.

VII   And Then

Two o'clock in the afternoon, four o'clock in the afternoon, twelve midnight, dawn. It was all the same.

A wooden door, painted gray like everything else in the building. A short ring at the door, and then . . . To the left was the living room of Jamila's house, with the chairs still folded up on the table, as if no one had thought of using them for a long time. Since when? Since the news arrived. And where was Yusra?

24

The martyr's wife lay on her bed, utterly broken, shaken by fits of weeping so intense that they took away all her strength. "How?" she shouted. "Why?" Faintness took hold of her from time to time, and the women would come to her, bringing rose water and eau de cologne, massaging her temples and her flushed face. Blackness is the sign of a martyr's wife, blackness rising up on all sides with the stammerings of the women calling for calm and patience. Her sudden sobbing shattered the stillness and they gathered round her trying to soothe her. Patience! Is there anything in death to be patient about?

Her dull eyes moved round the corners of the room, and the few pieces of simple furniture: the double-doored cupboard with its top loaded up with cases and bags, the chairs in a circle round the bed. In them were women, old and young, dressed in black. Concern, and sad silent contemplation.

In the midst of this Yusra lay on the bed in an agony of grief, her head on a square pillow with colored patterns of gold and silver flowers and oriental designs on the black silk of the pillow case—a present from Kuwait, made in Hong Kong.

They brought her orange-juice, but she refused to drink a drop. They pleaded with her, loving and insistent: "Yusra, you're going to have a child."

The child! What had he done wrong? Yusra drank a glass of juice, becoming more aware of the presence of the three-month-old child inside her. Quickly, decisively, she considered the matter. Three months in the womb. Six more to complete the pregnancy. Another person would be born. It would be a Palestinian, from its first moment in the world.

Yusra's mother tried to persuade her to stop her choking sobs and eat something. Everything, she told Yusra, is fate and chance: God decrees the span of each of our lives from the moment of our birth. It was enough that she, Yusra, had got out of Tal al-Zaatar and was still alive. Her mother also said something about a wall on which Yusra had stood and about the dozens of dogs scavenging among the bodies thrown at the foot. She talked about the need to go on with the living of her life.

Yusra screamed, her voice becoming louder; her swollen eyelids becoming redder:

"Don't talk to me about forgetting!"

Her mother leaned her worn face over her, her tears falling, her handkerchief tied round her chin in two strands that fell down on to her bosom. She stroked her daughter's hair. Yusra screamed again:

"Don't talk to me about forgetting!"

He was gazing at her, smiling out of the small photograph she'd immediately hung up on the opposite wall.

VIII Scenes

Beirut was like a box full of matches. It was transformed now into a vast land of volcanic ashes and flowing molten tar, and it was crumbling minute by minute. He hadn't liked Beirut, had been irritated by the heavy traffic there. "I was ill when I got back from India," he'd say. "I had a headache. For the first week my head wouldn't clear."

He'd fall silent and his thoughts would stray. "What's wrong, my dear?" I'd say. "What are you thinking about?"

"I was miles away," he'd say, and when I asked him where, he'd say: "the West Bank." I'd get horribly depressed sometimes because his thoughts were always there. He'd talk to me at length about his village and the days he'd spent there.

He loved taking photographs of natural scenes, and I'd say to him: "What sort of pictures are these? Take a picture of us!"

He loved Maghdusha. We went there and took pictures of ourselves among the trees, near the huge white statue of the Virgin which seems to rise up to Heaven on the spiral staircase that surrounds it.

Photographs of the sun descending from the gray clouds, like a red apple falling into the sea. White clouds flying at sunset, like locks of hair. Two lonely daisies in a field of green grass.

Anemones, wild thorns the color of violet, tarragon flowers and a statue of the Lady of Love, with tree-tops that seemed to embroider the fringes of Heaven.

I remember how he photographed a vine in a corner, with a natural scene stretched behind it. Then there was the child of Jamila—who got married after we left Tal al-Zaatar—his teeth not yet appeared, running happily in the grass. There was a picture of all of us together, our hands clasped beneath the huge lilac tree that cast its shadow on our faces. I was puzzled by the picture he took of his soldier's cap as it lay amid the grass and the flowers. How strange! What made him take a picture of a cap lying happily among the grasshoppers and small pebbles and roses? Just a soldier's cap? He used, too, to love taking pictures of the sun when it was close to the earth, at sunrise or sunset, and he always managed to capture its golden light, making me feel that everything linked to him overflowed with the shimmering light of a glimmering sunrise. Ahmad came from a town of olives and almonds, and he radiated joy; that's why, when I see pictures of him, he's always laughing.

The last time he visited me, I remember, I'd had a dream which I shall never forget. I dreamed that he and I were sleeping in our house, which was on a rock high up on the top of a mountain, with a deep valley beneath us. Asleep on this rock, we were about to fall, and the rock, huge but unsteady, was about to tumble down with us.

The dream unsettled me and I told him about it. "You're anxious about getting a house," he said. "We'll soon find one to live in."

Now I always see him in my dreams. The last time I saw him, he was asking me to heat some water so he could take a bath. The last bath he had was at the base, just before he met his death; but in my dream he asked me for hot water. I was wearing dark clothes, black on black, in mourning for him. I felt happy, and rejoiced; I was almost wild with happiness. I woke up, and knew it had all been a dream. My grief was unbearable.

The clothes I sleep in are as black as all the rest. I've forgotten many things but I still remember the white wedding dress we hired for his mother to take a picture of us.

The woman's pregnant and dressed in black. I am that woman in black. He was anxious for me and told me of his concern for me and the birth. "You really care for me that much?" I'd ask him tenderly. From the first month he started to plan for the upbringing of this child I now wait for alone.

When he died, I felt my life had ended, that everything had come to a stop at once and there was nothing left in the world.

I'll try to live . . . to fight against the sadness weighing down on my soul, leading me, sometimes, to feel that I'm losing my sanity. I'll try—but it's not easy at all.

But I will try.

When I remember, I weep. I open the album and look at the photographs. I come upon the sentence he wrote inside:

"These pictures make me feel I've become a professional—an expert photographer. I've taken them to embody phases of a life: phases of darkness, and phases of light. There are times of bitterness and there will be times of beauty and tenderness and light.

"Those times will come."

All I remember apart from that is his smile.

A Balcony
Over the Fakihani

Deux amours! Je puis mourir de l'amour terrestre, mourir de dévouement. J'ai laissé des âmes dont la peine s'accroîtra de mon départ! Vous me choisissez parmi les naufragés, ceux qui restent sont-ils pas mes amis?

Sauvez-les!

(Rimbaud, *Une Saison en Enfer*)

I. Su'ad

(1)

Why did my heart become troubled when the carpet plant grew so big?

It grew. It branched and grew tall till that day dawned. The little cutting my neighbor gave me flourished. Its heart-shaped leaves fanned out over the trellis, and on their green surface were red spots the color of blood, which spread like the memory of the nightmare I had: white dust and smoke, and, stretched out on the ground, a dead man I didn't know, his body gashed and spattered with blood. The plant grew bigger, spreading out in front of me, then, after a while, it turned to the color of wine. I laughed at my fears, heaved a deep sigh and grew calm.

I'd taken it from its small tin box and put it in an earthenware pot on the balcony, near the mimosa and sweet basil. The velvety leaves flourished until it became almost like a real wine-colored carpet furnishing a corner of the balcony.

The balcony of this apartment of ours in Fakihani was on the corner of the block, right opposite the Rahmeh Building. Jinan and I would sit there every afternoon, with the children close by inside playing house or watching the Sinbad series, and we'd tell one another our troubles, and talk about the high prices and the problems of life. We'd remember Amman, losing ourselves in our recollections; we hadn't been back there for many years, since Black September. We recalled my mother, friends, her family and relations, and Hajjeh Salimeh, whose death we learned of only from a brief letter. Umar would join us to drink lightly sweetened coffee, and we'd discuss our daily affairs with concealed bitterness or sarcastic comments. Umar was a natural humorist. He'd stretch out his hand towards Jinan, and his eyes would sparkle with merriment as she raised her own hand and laughingly slapped his. He'd make us roar with laughter, from the bottom of our hearts. Acquaintances or neighbors would drop in, and I'd bring chairs out from inside, moving, myself, to the old bedside table when the place had filled up.

Around us, in Fakihani, everything was swarming and full of noise: people milling about, voices, chaotic traffic. The gaze was held by narrow openings into rooms side by side with one another, piled high with trunks and possessions, lived in by families forced to migrate here from the South. In the street groups of youths playing with balls made out of cloth shouted to one another, among them Karim, who'd left school and started work at a printer's, but still sucked his thumb. Fighters in civilian dress, their revolvers at their sides, wandered through the narrow streets during their short leave from the bases, stopping briefly in front of the cigarette stalls and places selling soft drinks. Middle-aged women, their henna-dyed hair sparkling in the evening light, were gathered round a *nargila** on one of the balconies; behind them could be seen lines crammed with children's clothes and white diapers. Iraqi youths stood in the doorways of their crowded apartment buildings to exchange greetings and swap the latest news of party and regime. At one corner of the Rahmeh Building you could see Abu Fu'ad with his apron tied round his waist, cutting up cakes and sweetmeats and putting them on the front of his stall in pyramids like little hills.

Umar got ready to go out on his night patrol. He went over some rules of French grammar with the children and ate a few mouthfuls of endive with oil that I'd prepared for lunch. Noticing that the bread was running short, he went down to the grocer, Abu Muhammad, then called up: "Su'ad!" I looked down from the balcony and let

---

* *Nargila*: A kind of pipe in which the tobacco is drawn through water.

down a plastic bucket attached to a rope, into which he put a bag of bread and a jar of the red pepper paste he loved. Then he set off, and disappeared from view at the first bend in the alley. When I turned to go back inside, my eyes lit on the dark leaves of the carpet plant, which was now the color of lilac; but my mind went back to the dream.

(2)

I knew him before Black September. I'd see him some-times in military dress, with his Kalashnikov over his shoulder, talking to his friends in front of the office on Jabal al-Husain in Amman, then getting into the land-rover to go to the bases in the Jordan Valley. I learned by chance that people called him Umar the Tunisian, but didn't give much thought as to whether he came from Tunisia or whether it was a name used within the movement.

Umar . . . I took the name in almost unconsciously, like all the other new names around me. Most of the young men who joined the Resistance chose new names as a talisman, in memory of some hero or as a reminder of a certain place. The only name in the movement that really surprised me—I remember it to this day—was the name Sa'id Mahran, which I heard in the students' training camp near Baq'a camp. The person in charge asked us to form a line outside the camp, and we went over one at a time to give him the names we'd chosen. None of the girls, I remember, chose distinctive names, but the young men called out their various movement names loudly and enthusiastically: Izz al-Din al-Qassam, Nasser, Fahd, Guevara, Castro. Then the young man at the end of the

line came forward and said in a strong but quiet voice:
"Sa'id Mahran." At once I recalled the scene of Sa'id
Mahran leaving prison, in the novel by Naguib Mahfouz
which I'd borrowed from the school library. I didn't know
Umar then, and didn't notice him in any special way. He
was one of those fighters who disappear for a time, then
simply turn up; you don't realize they're there till they've
left again.

I saw him once more at the house of Im Mahmoud,
who lived next door to us in al-Husain camp, and whose
daughter, Latifa, was a friend of mine. Abu Mahmoud
had gone to Brazil after the Exodus, and when God
favored him and his trade flourished, he married and
settled down and had children there; all Im Mahmoud
received from him was a money order every two months.
From that time on she lived alone with her two children.
When the Resistance began, her house was always full of
young men and women fighting for the cause, and she
became a mother to all of them. The young men would
come to her hungry, tired, exhausted sometimes, and find
food, hot water for baths and glasses of tea. They called
her Yamma* and told her all about themselves, and about
any problems they had with family or girlfriends. I used to
go and see Latifa every day. We'd study together and help
get the food ready, kneading the dough before sending it
off to the baker's oven, or hollowing out zucchini and
eggplants. One day, when Im Mahmoud had prepared a
plate of *maftoul*, Umar came and sat on the floor and ate
with us. In his own country, he told us, the dish was called
couscous. Im Mahmoud brought him a cushion to lean

* *Yamma* means "mother" in popular Palestinian dialect.

against, and conversation turned to the kind of food eaten in our two countries, and then to the state of affairs in his country. He'd joined the Resistance, he said, after being a student in the Department of Political Science at the Sorbonne. I gathered he couldn't go back to his country because of proscribed political activity.

That was before September. The day before the September events, Latifa and I went to the Musarwa Quarter, a poor district at the back of Jabal Amman, to help with civil defense and first aid. After twenty days of gunfire and injuries the Jordanian army still hadn't managed to occupy the quarter after entering Jabal Amman. After the fighting Latifa and I went back to Jabal al-Husain, wearing long peasant dresses so as not to be recognized at the road blocks. I saw him again on the few occasions he came to Im Mahmoud's house, and discovered that when he was absent for a long time I was full of anxiety and expectation; I began to miss his friendly presence and feel the need to see him. The last time he stood in front of the porcelain sink near the doorway washing his face, and I ran to fetch a towel for him from the bathroom. He wiped his face and opened his eyes; then he asked me if I'd marry him. I felt confused and uncomfortable, not because he'd asked me, but because of what my family might say. When I plucked up the courage to tell them, my mother gave her consent, but my father was more reluctant. He spoke of the difficult conditions in the country following the events of September. This man was a *fida'i*, he said; what settled future could he hope for? After the Resistance had retreated from the Woods of Jarash and 'Ajloun, I received a letter from Umar in Beirut, asking me to join him there. Again, my mother supported me. I packed what clothes I had, and, with God's help, set out for Beirut.

(3)

Beirut!

Great, sinuous mountains suddenly appeared, and, spread out behind them, the broad, sparkling sea. From a distance this expanse of sea, rimmed by the horizon, seemed a thing totally distinct from the huge, outspread city that plunged into it like an arrow. It was the first time in my life that I'd seen the sea, and I was amazed by the strange shape it took on as it gathered itself round the city. I phoned Umar, who came to pick me up at the taxi station, and for the moment I stayed with some friends of his who lived at al-Rawsha.* I hadn't expected the city to be so beautiful—the blue sea and the tall buildings and the sidewalk cafes full of customers. In the evening we'd go for a stroll down the long Corniche among hundreds of other walkers, and buy some hamburgers and beer. We'd stop for a while in front of the Rawsha rock. "This isn't one rock," I said once, "it's two. Did it get its name because it looks like just one rock from a distance?" He laughed. "The rock's famous for suicides," he said. "No one who wants to commit suicide cares whether there's one rock or two." We'd walk among the bright lights and the cars, and I'd tell him how surprised I was to see so many people out at night. "To see all these people," I'd say, "you'd think everyone in the city had come out for a walk." He'd pull me towards him and put his arm round

---

* Al-Rawsha is a seafront district of West Beirut. It was once prosperous and noted for its elegant cafes and restaurants.

39

me, and we'd go on. I didn't dare tell him how embarrassed I felt to have him so close to me in front of all these people. But though I was stiff and tense, he was relaxed and at ease. He talked to people whether he knew them or not, joked with shopkeepers and working girls and neighbors, and replied in fluent French to anyone who came up and spoke to him in that language.

During the day they all went out, and I was left alone. I'd take a book and read a page or two, then jump up, unable to concentrate; there were so many new things all around me, and I couldn't take them all in as yet. I'd fill in the hours by dusting and devising unnecessary cleaning jobs in the apartment, and when I'd gone round and round without finding anything to do, I used to go out on the balcony overlooking the sea and lie in the sun. The sun seemed fresh and gentle at first, then I'd feel its concentrated heat on my body. I'd close my eyes, seeing just the color of orange through my eyelids; so the blue water of the sea was outside, and, within my eyes, a bright sandy beach.

The first week was taken up with the small parties we gave in the evening. Lots of friends would come with food and drink, and we'd all sit in a big circle on the floor, swapping jokes and comments and singing the songs of Shaikh Imam.* The evening would end with music and traditional songs, finishing, often, with *maijana*† verses like "how beautiful you are, oh violet, in the springtime of our land."

---

* Shaikh Imam is a contemporary Egyptian poet and singer, associated with popular protest songs.
† A *maijana* is a very old folk song, associated with such countries as Palestine, Jordan, Lebanon and Syria.

Since the people we were staying with weren't married, and staying with them any longer would have meant constraints on both sides, we had to move and find a home of our own. With the help of friends we rented a sixth-floor apartment—in the Mazra'a district, as I remember—with three rooms containing only a foam mattress on the floor and a few pots and pans. In the mornings the aroma of fresh coffee floated up from our coffee pot, and we'd follow the coffee just with two glasses of milk for breakfast. Then helplessness, for both of us! After Umar's allowance of 250 liras had been used for the rent, we were penniless, and we just couldn't find a job for me to do; I was doing voluntary work training people on first aid courses, but I needed something that would bring in money. My God, the whole situation was becoming such a maze of difficulties that a trip to the moon seemed straightforward by comparison! You had to give tens of thousands of liras to get a work permit issued to you, and I even heard that some Lebanese, like those from al-Hermel and Akkar, couldn't get permits because their national status was still under discussion. The Palestinian offices were full of people coming in from Jordan, and in any case there were only a few limited jobs there. I didn't know what to do. We had to leave the apartment because we couldn't afford the rent, and searched around until we came across two small rooms, originally intended for the caretaker of the block, for 100 liras a month. All right, we said at first, if it's a caretaker's apartment, we'll just have to put up with it. But when we settled in . . . well, I can hardly describe what it was like. There were people banging at the door to ask about renting apartments, or coming at all hours of the day and night and asking for the apartments of people they wanted to visit. The place was like an oven because the walls and ceiling were covered with the pipes for the central heating, there were no windows and the only door, apart from the main door, was a small one at the back of the block opening on to an area strewn with piles of garbage and rats' nests. But none of this mattered. The main thing was the cheap rent.

The first day I was delighted; I've got a home at last, I said, and enthusiastically set about cleaning and tidying and dusting it. But as time went on—the next day, and the day after that, and the day after that—life became a nightmare. Sweat poured from our bodies, even though it was the depths of winter, the room got like a sooty chimney if we so much as smoked a couple of cigarettes, and at night the humidity was so oppressive that we felt as if a paving stone was pressing down on our chests. We'd wake up exhausted and aching in every limb.

We had to keep the light on all the time, and could only tell night from day by going out to the front of the building. I started coughing all the time, and my face turned a yellow color, like cumin; and when we went to the doctor we were told, to our astonishment, that I was pregnant. My first thought was that I'd give birth without my mother at my side. Umar, though, was very happy and cheerful; he lost his frown, and started smiling and laughing just as he used to before we left Amman. He'd try to stop me tiring myself with housework, and carry the heavy washbowl for me and put food in front of me, insisting that I should eat more than usual. "There are two of you now, not one," he'd say with a smile.

But one day I went to the bathroom, and found blood

streaming out from between my legs. I didn't tell him; it was a temporary problem, I told myself, which would go away before too long. Then it got worse and we had to go to the University Hospital. I don't remember much about it, but I do have a vivid memory of coming home with a feeling of defeat, carrying a long prescription for drugs and vitamins. It wasn't just a matter of losing the baby, it was anemia too, and I was told I needed fresh air. He became frantic, and said we must move at once, without a moment's delay. Then, a few days before we found somewhere new to live, we heard people banging violently on the door in the middle of the night. Umar picked up his revolver, then flung open the door suddenly, so as to take them by surprise. They were from the security forces. "I know who you are!" he shouted. "I'm not letting you in!" They didn't answer, but simply took him off to the police station on the grounds that the apartment was being used to store arms. Then they burst in and searched the place inch by inch, even though they'd examined our identity cards and Umar's permit for carrying firearms.

(4)

Shatila Camp.

We lived in the middle of the camp near a girl's primary school, a yellow UNRWA* school building with a line of washbasins in the yard outside, from which a depressing, sour smell of watery milk hit you as you passed by.

Our home was in a three-story block housing dozens

* United Nations Relief and Works Agency.

of families, with a long balcony on each floor that formed
a corridor on to which individual rooms opened.

Shatila! People would greet one another in the morning and evening and would talk without any kind of
ceremony or introduction, in a Palestinian accent as au-
thentic as if they'd arrived in Beirut just the day before;
and their homes were fitted out in a makeshift way, as if
they were going to set off again the next morning.

There was light and air in Shatila, but it was criss-
crossed by thousands of drains with dark brown moss on
the edge of them, flowing with dirty washing water that
had pieces of garbage floating on it; these we'd jump over,
or cross on wooden boards or bits of metal, depending on
the particular place. I started to get to know a few people
and recognize their faces, and I began to go with the other
women to the Sabra souk to buy vegetables and things for
the house, bargaining with the traders who came round
with their carts. God, how cheap things were then! For
ten liras I used to buy everything I needed for a couple of
days, and 30 liras would cover fruit and vegetables and
meat for a whole week. What do 100 liras buy now? Such
a ridiculous amount you might just as well never have
bought it, or seen it, or known anything about it.

I started to make new friends. There was Husniyyeh, a
young married woman who spent most of the night
washing pants and shirts for her laundryman husband.
And Im Salman, who never stopped laughing and had a
thousand proverbs to hand, one for every occasion.
There'd be constant daily quarrels between her and the
family of her husband, who was away working in the Gulf,
because she neglected her eight children during his ab-
sence; she'd leave things to her eldest daughter, who was

ten years old, and spend her time chattering and gossiping in all the different houses she called at. Then there was Im Hamdi, who lived in the room next to ours. Her husband worked as a driver in one of the Resistance organizations, while she cared for her six children, of whom the youngest suffered from polio. She was tall with a rather dark complexion, and no one ever heard her moan or complain. She always used to help me out with things, especially when I was pregnant and eventually gave birth to twins—a boy and a girl, Ruba and Jihad. And then there was Jinan, who was always coming to see me to help her meet the women of the block and invite them to a discussion or celebration organized by the Women's Union. I'd known her for a long time, but we'd never had the chance before to sit down and have the kind of talk that refreshed the soul. I was busy with two babies and she was always occupied with her own interests.

May 1973—and tank gun and machine gun fire on Shatila camp. There were no shelters in the camp, so people fled to Sabra, where they hid in the doorways of buildings or in warehouses. He came at night and took me away. The sky was lit with green and red stars, and the thunder and lightning wasn't real thunder and lightning, but bullets from machine guns and small arms. We were running and stumbling, carrying the two babies, bottles of milk and bags of clothes and diapers. He left me at the house of someone we knew in the Jadid Road, then went away again. The Lebanese army tanks came to Cola Roundabout and began to shell the camps; the building shook, and the constant din was like the noise of an earthquake swallowing up heaven and earth together. Next morning, as I was giving Ruba some milk, I noticed

45

a white hair in the middle of her head. I couldn't believe a baby's hair could turn white.

When things had quietened down, we went back to the camp, where the neighborhood women gathered together, each one talking about the things that had happened to her. When Im Hamdi lifted up the two children, she noticed the white hair on Ruba's head, and, although she didn't ask me about it, her face changed and she let out a scream. I didn't realize at first that it was her voice. As she cried out and wailed, the neighbors were astonished to hear the voice of the woman who was always so silent, and the men came out of the neighboring rooms in their pajamas and undershirts. I didn't know what to do; words stuck in my throat and I had to fight back my tears. I hugged her, unable to speak, and her children ran forward to take my own. It was as if what had happened had happened only to us.

The days passed, disrupted by our move to Damascus as a result of Umar's work. In Yarmouk camp there, life went on slowly and quietly, and during this time he traveled abroad several times on training courses. Time! I was never aware of time there; it used to repeat itself in the same way every day, from morning to evening. I was busy looking after the children, except for those few fleeting moments you capture before falling asleep, when I'd think of my mother and father, and of my sister who, I heard, had been married, but whose wedding I couldn't attend because of problems with the Jordanian secret police. I recalled Jordan and the days in Amman. I'll never forget the *fida'i* who was in the same shared taxi from Jarash camp to Amman. We were stopped at the police check at the Sports Stadium crossroads and were asked to show our identity cards; and after we'd handed them over, they came back and ordered the young man to get out to be searched. He was wearing civilian clothes—no one wore combat gear any more after September. He was twenty at most, and I was sure, when he gazed at me with his eyes shining meaningfully, that he was one of the fighters. His left hand moved towards his lower back; I understood at once, and whispered: "Give it to me." Quickly and quietly he slipped his hand from his jacket to the leather seat and placed a mass of cold metal in my hand. I took it at once and tucked it under my dress, then dropped it into my handbag. When they searched him, they found nothing. He took his revolver back from me before we reached the Abdali taxi station in Amman, and I remember with total clarity his entreating gaze and the flash of gratitude that appeared in his black eyes.

(5)

Return to Beirut!

Beirut. Fakihani. It was the end of 1978, and there was bustle and overcrowding and a strange sense of familiarity, as though the place was a piece of home. Cries and conversations would flit from one balcony to the next, as if each balcony was actually a part of the other houses. Jinan and I would sit on our balcony every afternoon, chatting away as if to make up for all the days when we'd found no time to talk; she'd finish her work, and I'd go and sit with her when I'd come back from the clinic and done some household chores. I'd managed—at last!—to find a job in Beirut. We'd make coffee in a big pot and try and keep it covered with a saucer so it didn't get cold. Then we'd pour cup after cup and exchange memories and news. Umar came sometimes and joined us in our coffee and talk; he'd laugh at us when we complained, and say we were making too much of things. "It's not the end of the world, girls," he'd say. "You've got to show what you're made of." He'd tell one of his jokes or make some remark, and we'd roar with laughter, from the bottom of our hearts.

We'd be disturbed sometimes by things that happened around us. The eyes of neighbors would peer out to see who our visitors were, or check how clean the washing was that was spread out on the line, or how many pots of mimosa or basil there were. Sometimes the young men were called out at night, and the buzz of conversation or the clicking of weapons would come up over the balcony and settle on the blankets and sheets that covered us as we slept; and when a civil or military vehicle went by, the grating of its wheels and the roar of its engine as it careered on its way would come right into the room. Endearments or abuse would reach our apartment as soon as they reached the ears of the people they were meant for. But I felt no reason to complain; everything was fine as long as we were together. When I lived in Damascus, there was peace and quiet, but he was so often away too. Here he was with me, we were together, sharing the responsibilities for the children, of whom there were now four. It was he who wanted the last one; the pregnancy had come about by mistake, but he didn't encourage me to have an abortion, asking me instead what I had against a large family. I respected his wishes, realizing how much he longed for his own family that he hadn't seen for so many years. And in a strange way, the face of the little baby, Jumana, was like his.

One day, suddenly, Umar fell ill, and his health collapsed all at once. He'd spend a lot of time in bed, coughing endlessly, and we moved him to the hospital and arranged for him to have some tests. The doctors suspected something wrong with the heart, but they couldn't pin down exactly what was wrong and advised him to go abroad for treatment.

And so Umar went away.

II. Umar

(1)

In the first few days after I left, I'd remember her exactly as she'd looked at the moment of parting: confused and laughing in a way that was rather like weeping, darting and urgent in her movements like the water of a babbling mountain spring. I took her chin in my hand and raised it, so as to place a kiss on her forehead. "Just a moment," she said, "wait a second." For a moment or two she went inside as if everything was as usual, as though I wasn't going away at that very moment. The child in her arms started crying. Friends came up to ask me to hurry because the car was waiting at the corner of the street by the main road; and there was the sound of its horn reminding me as it swept over the shops opposite and came in through the balcony. She came up, and I took little Jumana from her, pressed her to me and kept on kissing the children till Abu Antun pulled me away. "Hurry up," he said, "we want you to get better and come back. You can hear the car's waiting." She waved from the balcony: I saw her gentle face and the white kerchief she used for

49

gathering up her hair, and the hem of her simple dress sweeping down behind. "The cigarettes!" she shouted at the top of her voice, not noticing the look of amazement on the face of Abu Mahmoud the shopkeeper as he looked up at her, then realized she wasn't calling to him this time. "The cigarettes," she said. "Don't forget!"

As for me, the car took me off, and I didn't forget; I kept on seeing her, as if I'd never been away before. I'd never, on any journey, been as sick at heart as I was now.

I remembered, too, how once she was wearing a wine-colored wrap as she called to me, smiling at me, sitting on a cane chair with her back to the shelves made out of planks and red bricks, posing for a picture to be taken. Suddenly she jumped up and said: "Wait . . . just a moment."

A moment . . . The doorbell . . . The neighbors asking for their bowl.

A moment passed, and I waited for her to come back, filling in the time by looking at the things on the shelves. I focused the camera on the curios I was so used to seeing there, but didn't press the button. There were Japanese dolls with slender pins in their hair, which little Jumana loved and whispered to as if they were real living human beings, a wooden eagle from the Caucasus which I'd brought back from a training course, African gods made from stiff reed stalks decorated with red beads and colored necklaces, pieces of Cuban handicraft, a Chinese porcelain cat leaning over a jug of milk, books in Arabic and French, and a steel bust of Lenin.

I gazed at them and waited for her.

After a while she came, pulling back the fringe of the wine-colored wrap with its embroidered golden threads.

Smiling, she sat down again for the picture to be taken, and this time I put her in the frame, oblivious to everything around her. I was fascinated by the sudden slight smile, by the merriment and suppressed desire for life that showed around her dimpled cheeks. I discovered her face once more where the lines in the circular lens crossed: the wheat-colored complexion and the black eyes that sparkled so alluringly the moment the smile spread beyond the clear line of her lips. A woman had been living with me for years, and now I felt like someone discovering for the first time that this woman was a woman before she was my wife, that she was something molded from the clay of life just as the springtime soil is planted with seedlings. Was this just a poetic fancy? Perhaps. I'd begun to lose touch with reality from the moment the doctors had discovered my illness. A thin needle was pushed into my arm; I became totally drowsy and the muscles in my shoulders begin to twitch convulsively. What I saw before me, with utter clarity, was the trace of the smile still lingering on her face when it had returned to its normal serious expression after the picture had been taken.

We stopped at the door. On the landing were the ceaseless footsteps of the neighbors going up and down, and we were constantly disturbed by the voices of their children as they tumbled over one another in their fights in the entrance. She was anxious to make me feel everything was normal, as if I was just going off on my nightly patrol and not on an urgent journey for medical treatment. And a frightening journey it was, because it was an emergency, and a shock for someone who, all his life, had been accustomed to good health. In her confusion she came impulsively towards me and wanted to embrace me;

then she became embarrassed because of the people around and laughed abruptly, with a sound like the water of a gurgling spring that stops as suddenly as it begins to gush. It was more like a kind of sob.

The cigarettes, she'd said. Don't forget.

She didn't want me to smoke, and I stubbed out the cigarette in the tiny square tray provided between the seats of the plane. Then I gazed at the curtain that hung between us and the cockpit. A draught ruffled the middle of it, and it blew towards us as the plane climbed steeply. The "No smoking" sign went out, and we were now allowed to light cigarettes and smoke them as long as we wanted, until a few minutes before touchdown. I looked at my neighbor's head which was glued to the top of the seat he was leaning back on, and I arranged my camera so that it wouldn't slip off my lap without my noticing it. What did these women understand about life? Be careful, they always say. Just a moment. Don't smoke. Don't drink. A long list of weird and wonderful don'ts! A joke came back to me, and I laughed audibly to myself. The man next to me, who was going abroad on a scholarship, stirred in his seat. "What's the joke?" he asked. Choking back the rest of my laughter and lighting a fresh cigarette, I told him. "A man went to the Party and said he wanted to become a loyal member. The members accepted him and told him he had to stick to the rules. 'No smoking,' they said. 'Okay,' said the man. 'And no drinking.' 'Fair enough,' he said. 'And mind you don't go chasing after women.' 'Of course not,' he said, shaking his head. 'Will you sacrifice your life without question if required to?' they asked. 'You bet I will,' the man burst out. 'What life is there left after all?'" I laughed, and the student laughed

too, showing his gold front teeth. Then he fell comfort-
ably asleep again, and I was left alone with the drone of
the engines and the rings of black smoke coming out from
beneath the wings.

Sooner or later, we'd reach the place where I was to be
treated—the final link in the chain that had begun with a
sharp pain in the chest and would end with what people
always refer to as a white hospital bed. As a matter of fact,
these beds aren't really white, but only the patients who
sleep in them know that. I tried to imagine the hospital,
remembering how a comrade who was treated there once
described it. Old hags, he'd told me, pressing the pages of
the daily newspaper between his wasted hands, nothing
but old hags as far as the eye could see. He'd said that the
sight of these women, with their flabby skin and gray hair
and bare toothless gums had left him with an abiding
hatred of the female sex for a very long time afterwards.
Just imagine, he'd say, they ride exercise bicycles and
push their skinny thighs about with a strength and gusto
that would make you jealous to see. To the sanatorium,
then—to the end of the world.

(2)

On the outside the sanatorium was shaped like a seven-
pointed star. Inside it was like a military establishment,
equipped to provide everything except repose. It strikes
me that a hospital, any hospital, is like a prison: even
though the aims of the place are finally different, you find
the same kind of rooms, the same kind of machinery and
equipment sometimes, and sometimes the same restric-
tions on freedom too. Hospitals smell of ether, cotton

wool and disinfectant, while prisons reek of dampness and decay, carried on gusts of air laden with the concentrated sulphurous smell of latrines. Both hospital and prison give you a sense of shock when you go in and a feeling of joy when you come out. You go in and then wait, for hour after hour and day after day. Then, all at once, the gates open up to just two alternatives: death or life—wheat or barley, as my mother always says, or boy or girl, as my wife always says. Whenever I remembered her, I was struck by what seemed like a tremor in my heart, like a fluttering butterfly which would almost take wing, then suddenly sink down like a heavy stone.

Anxiety! I'd wander through the corridors and the X-ray rooms and the examination rooms, a wandering that became more frantic as my temperature shot up, and went on rising as if nothing would ever stop it.

Examinations were ordinary routine ones at first, then they become critical and complicated. Pain, pain I could do nothing to stop, tore through every fiber of my body; there were pale, ghastly faces all around me, while my mind was full of the memories of my friends, Jamal, Zuhdi, Abu Antun, Hamid, François—I couldn't recall their features in detail, but I saw them at the back of my mind as I tossed and turned in the furnace of my bed.

Fever! I couldn't stand the doctor who was in charge of my case; I hated her so much I didn't know how to endure it. Right from the start I was irritated by the domineering way she spoke to the nurses and her arrogance towards the patients as she moved from bed to bed; and then they moved me to the recovery room, where she was in charge of my treatment. I was flat on my back with a raging temperature, and I hated her. For me she was just a white uniform like the rest of the nurses, except that she was taller and had a forbidding expression on her face.

My temperature rose still further, and I no longer knew what was going on around me. I felt a sense of total separation from my body, I was fainting away, with a raging thirst inside like thorns tearing at me. I lost all sense of time; all I knew about, now and again, was the white drops of serum dripping into my veins. Thirst and fever and fainting. I must have raved. I opened eyes blocked with sand and found the doctor standing in front of me, shouting at the nurse who was sitting on the chair by the side of my bed. She spoke several times to the nurse in her own language, and the nurse left, while she stayed with me. She noticed, with surprise, that I was conscious, then sadly shook her head and told me in French that she'd dismissed the nurse because she'd dozed off several times when she was supposed to be watching over me. Things faded again and thick clouds gathered over me. Where was I? Where was I?

One morning, I don't remember exactly when, the darkness that covered my eyes fell away from me, and I woke to find her standing by my bed. "That's good," she said. "Your temperature's dropped; you've started to get better." She helped me get out of bed and go to the window, where I saw that the world outside was covered with a blanket of white snow. In spite of my exhaustion I found the strength to thank her briefly. A slender thread of vitality was stirring within my feeble limbs and shattered body. She replied that I needn't be grateful; she was only doing her duty. We began to exchange a little conversation sometimes.

When they took me out of the recovery room and back

to my own room, she visited me every day and showed satisfaction at the progress I was making. She checked the results of my medical tests and took me along to see the physiotherapist; medicine alone wasn't enough, she said, and she tried to get me to follow all kinds of therapy. She told me the results of the test, saying that the type of infection discovered in the laboratory was unknown in their country. No, I wasn't suffering from any kind of heart disease, and it wasn't tuberculosis or cancer; a new kind of infection, previously unknown to them, had been eating away at the lung cells and destroying them. I was from the Middle East, I told her jokingly, and that explained everything. She laughed, then we talked, and went on and on talking. I began to get used to her, and a special kind of familiarity sprang up between us.

She told me I was going to get better, and I was filled with the sense of gentle joy known only to those who are restored to good health after disease has reduced them almost to skin and bone. Louisa assured me I would get better, and she invited me to have dinner at the weekend at a restaurant near the hospital.

Good health, I thought, as I got myself ready, was a crown on the brows of the healthy, visible only to the sick. After forty consecutive days in the hospital, I was going to leave it for a few hours.

I thought of her as I walked down the great staircase that led to the exit. I'd told her all about my life, about my wife and children and the kind of work I did, and she wasn't bored, but rather eager to hear more. Talk to me, she'd say; and I'd talk to her at length, recalling the faces and features of loved ones, and friends, and stories about the children, and the news that Su'ad had sent me, lost in a glow of nostalgia for all the things I longed for. As time went on I began to feel that the contentment flowing through me didn't come just from the things we talked about or from the pangs of exile. It was Louisa as well; it was her, and the warmth of our friendship. A lot of people, she kept saying to me, are revolutionaries to start with, but then they get bored and find they can't keep it up. You're different from them, she said. You've still kept the vision that sees things afresh. The flower hasn't lost its fragrance.

I saw her waiting for me in the snow-covered court-yard. She was wearing a fur coat, and her smooth hair, which had always been tied in a bun, now fell loose on to her shoulders. Her cheeks were pink and the glimmer of her violet eyes shone like stars. My God, how was it possible? The doctor friend had become a seductive young gipsy girl, standing there amid the world of nature like a gazelle that roams among the trees and snow. Grace shone from her, and there was a smile on her lips. She put out her hand to take my arm, and we walked and talked as though we'd known one another since child-hood. There I truly saw her for the first time. Perhaps if I hadn't seen her there, at that moment, I wouldn't have loved her afterwards.

We went out together often after that, and devotion turned to love of a strange new kind, as strange as the close friendship that had linked us before. Time stood still, and the illness receded. Events conspired to provide us with places where we could be constantly together. When she'd finished her work, she'd hurry to be with me, and we'd sit and tell one another things, the most impor-tant or the most trifling, with the enthusiasm of those striving to bring back the memories of past times, not realizing that marvels are still possible. As I woke in the morning, my first thoughts, flashing before my mind like an arrow, would be: how was it possible, how could I love her so much, so very much? I never wondered why. Love's the last thing in the world that makes you wonder why. Once we went to a restaurant in the city center, and spent an evening by dim candle-light alongside a wedding party that happened to be taking place there that evening. There were cries of delight, and people clapping to the rhythm of the music, and bride and groom embracing, the bride shimmering in white and pink. And Louisa was with me.

It was like being in a dream with your eyes open—but my eyes really were fully open and awake. I knew exactly where I was, and knew, too, that it would all pass away as suddenly as it had begun. One day I'd go back, and it would be as if I'd never met her and loved her, as if I'd never known her in my life.

Louisa! She was thirty years old, with skin like snow and lips like wine. There was poetry in her, and music, and a gipsy's fingertips to touch the strings and turn them to raging fire. And my days with Louisa were to go on until my treatment was over. I went with her to her friends' parties. I went to her home to be introduced to her parents. While the world outside was covered with snow, we'd listen again and again, round an open fire, to the melodies of Theodorakis and the songs of Jacques Brel, and she introduced me, too, to the amazing music of Zamphir. I could never have believed an instrument like the flute was capable of expressing, at the same time, such sadness and such loneliness and such floods of untrammeled joy. In her country, she explained, music was a mirror of nature, and indeed it seemed to be like nature itself. Before I met Louisa I never used to bother to learn anything about the countries I was visiting; I was like someone on a military mission, who familiarizes himself with what he needs to carry out his task and leaves it at that. My own task here had been to get well and then move on; but now here I was, getting to know streets and food and cafés and people I met—even little nuances began to attract my attention. I described my life at home to her in minute detail, and she got to know the names of my family and friends, and became familiar with our political situation. She asked me to translate the letters I received, and it was as if she herself had become a member of the family.

Our happiness never lost its freshness; yet time was passing, and as my stay there drew towards its close, Louisa began to avoid meeting me in the eye. If I caught her avoiding my gaze, the violet eyes would darken suddenly, and be rimmed with a somber moistness that would take on the aspect of some strange, glimmering twilight. When I asked her what the matter was, she avoided all discussion of the subject, talking instead about the most unexpected things. She'd go to the shops with me, gaily pointing out shoes for my daughter or a coat for my son, or look around to find the most beautiful shawl for my wife. And other things too: the finest, most attractive embroidered tapestries for the house, or a really smart leather jacket just in my style. Then she took me to the flower shop to find some special small wild flowers, orange and reddish, peeping out through the shining cellophane paper. These, she told me, wouldn't wither after I'd taken them back; they were completely natural, and yet they'd never fade. She took a few days leave and went buzzing around like a bee from morning to night, searching out places I hadn't visited, natural sights or museums I hadn't known before, and looking for more presents to send back with me. Louisa, I'd say, you've done enough now; and she'd silence me with a light wave of the hand. It was as if she didn't want to invite talk of our coming separation, fearful of destroying the cocoon of dreams within which we'd lived so long.

Louisa; the reality and the dream. How was it possible? She plunged with me into joyful anticipations of my welcome home and their happiness at my return. They'd see how completely cured I was; the infection could have been fatal, but I'd fought through and recovered. She didn't talk about herself. It was as if she'd vanish in an instant the moment I'd gone, or be swallowed up by a crevice in the earth as if she'd never existed. All right, then; let it be so.

We chose to spend the last night away from the hospital, at a remote hotel nestling in the snow like an abandoned log on the edge of the forest. We had dinner at a restaurant built in the style of an old hunting lodge, and a violinist came right up to our table and played a rhapsody that used to be played for lovers in Hungary. For my part, I looked down and followed the movements of the throbbing bow with eyes that had ceased, for so long now, to hold any tears. But she wept for me; she shed tears in that small room which should be the dream of any pair of lovers. Yet wasn't I right to act as I did? What a mockery of a farewell it would have been if I'd wept as she did. She tried to apologize for her tears, and

said, in a breaking voice, that she would have followed me
to the end of time.

(3)

It was as if I'd come from another world. I altered my
watch to local time as soon as I landed. The noise of the
airport, the porters rushing to offer to carry my bag, the
hordes of boys selling chewing gum, or suddenly spring-
ing up next to the cars lined up outside: it all made me
realize I'd been transported back to a totally different
world.

On the way from the airport I looked at the old, drab
buildings as if seeing them for the first time. I don't know
why people, when they're abroad, think Beirut's the most
beautiful place in the world; it's not like that at all. The
disfigurements on its face had increased: from the bombing of buildings, from the garbage piled up by the sides of
the streets, and from the claustrophobic press of people
and vehicles that had come into being when war reduced
the city's living space. Before we reached our quarter, the
road passed by the Martyrs' Cemetery at the entrance to
the city, where the martyrs lie buried amid white marble
gravestones and wreaths of dried flowers. Whenever I
passed close to them, it seemed to me that they were
silently protesting: Why? Why did we have to die when we
wanted to live? It's something I prefer not to think about
too much. In Cairo, after leaving the airport, you go
through a huge quarter seething with humanity, called
Qarafa, and you soon realize that it's simply a cemetery
where people are living. In Cairo the living resort to the
tombs of the dead to go on living. Here the dead rest on

ground strewn with dried plants, to ensure that what caused their deaths will never happen again.

Our quarter, Fakihani—and I saw them again at last. It was as if I'd been away from them for many years. Whenever I asked about Jamal—how was he and when would he come and see us?—Su'ad changed the subject and moved on to something else; she talked about many things, but said nothing about him. But friends came and told me: Jamal's dead, didn't you know? How could I have known when I'd been away? So this was the tragedy she'd been trying to hide from me so as not to upset me straight after my return. My friend Jamal had met his death in the South. A mine had exploded during a reconnaissance and the lower part of his body had been shattered. He'd lain on the ground in his own blood, and hadn't wanted his comrades to get him to safety, calling out to them that it was no use and that he'd be dead within a few minutes. As the heavy enemy fire opened up on them, he told them to withdraw, and when they did manage to get to him it was all over. Jamal, a young man not yet twenty-five years old, wasn't there any more. I'd known him and loved him, and hadn't expected to lose him so soon. Perhaps, to be frank, I hadn't expected him to show such fortitude in the last moments of his ordeal. I heard, too, about comrades who'd abandoned the fight and gone off to a safer place. And that was what really surprised me: not Jamal's death in action, but those who'd left us. Yet life still goes on. What have we really gained when we give up the struggle and bow our heads?

The life I went back to was no longer the life I'd known; thanks to an infuriating medical report, which stated that I had to lead a quiet life from now on, I was given an administrative post. Reluctantly I had to accept this situation, tiresome though it was. But whenever it began to get me down, the thought came to me: Louisa. You're going to get well, she'd said. Then I'd feel a sense of inner joy, as though I was flitting along on the wings of a butterfly. I didn't try to forget her. What would happen to us if we forgot those dearest to us? I'd talk about her to Su'ad and Jinan, and felt that this cooled my longing for her—a crazy longing I'd never known before, but which I had to admit was there. I saw her everywhere, stretching out her hand to point at something, with that captivating smile on her face. I received letters from her, and wrote back asking her not to raise again the idea of coming to visit me here. It was out of the question, I said, and would remain so till the end of time.

When the three of us—Su'ad, Jinan and myself—were together, we'd joke about it. But when I was alone with Su'ad, she'd weep and say she couldn't get used to someone else being so strangely important. Then I'd hug her and ask her why she was afraid, and assure her that it meant nothing to me. Yet I feared for myself, and feared this crazy longing, even though I knew well enough that the whole thing was over once and for all, for ever.

One night Su'ad stirred in her sleep and woke shaking in every limb. I tried to calm her, and asked her what the matter was. "The dream," she said. "What dream?" I asked. "The two of us were in a cramped room," she said, "with a small window in one wall, and you flew out of the window and left me all alone." I gave her a hug, and she snuggled up to me like a frightened child. I tried to calm her, and, as always, swore to her that the matter with Louisa meant nothing to me at all. She nodded, then said, her face pale: "I know. It's something else I'm afraid of."

I was too utterly exhausted to be able to give any thought to her fears. I put my arm around her and told her to go to sleep.

III. Jinan

(1)

Morning, in this district of deafening traffic. There was the tramp of people passing, and the assortment of small stalls on the two sides of the alley, and the strong smell of the sun, and the ancient quinine trees covering the city playground. I left the entrance to the University. Snatches of conversation mingled on the sidewalk with songs being played on the handcarts that sold cassettes and the din of the machines with which workmen were mending a near-by street. On the ground, pushed to the sides by the wind and the shoes of people passing, were little blotches of yellow sand from the stack of sandbags used to protect the entrances of buildings and shops during the Phalangist bombardment in April and May. Su'ad had told me, the day before, that all the sandbags had been taken away, even from the hairdresser's salon of our neighbor Mustafa. It's incredible, sister, she said. The moment I opened my eyes, at seven this morning, I saw a line of girls waiting in front of the salon!

There were magazines and newspapers scattered about on the sidewalk, but I didn't stop to read the headlines; I'd be seeing it all at the office in a couple of hours' time. Reading just the headlines, without the story, always makes me feel oddly alarmed. I can read all about it at the office, and I'm not alone there either, so why poison the system first thing in the morning? There was smoke rising from a small shaft in the middle of the stove where the old black man was selling roasted peanuts. The clothes for the new season were in the shop windows, and the vendors had their boxes of fruit and vegetables out in front of them. There were the small violet eggplants with white streaks, called *sahouri* after Bait Sahour,* which I hadn't seen here before. My mother used to wait for them to come in in the summer and always made a special point of buying them. She'd make particular dishes with them whose names I've forgotten, and which I haven't tasted since we left the West Bank. I bought some of them, without really knowing what to do with them. The coarse paper bag they were sold in chafed the usual sensitive place on the palm of my hand, and I remembered how, some years earlier, I'd get off the bus from Abu Dis to go to the souk at the Khan al-Zayt Gate in the Old City of Jerusalem, where I used to buy things for my mother under the shaded arcades. I'd haggle with the traders, and they'd lower their prices and say: all right, you clever girl, just for you, how much do you want? Before long the small bag I was carrying would be bursting with the things I'd bought, and I'd start counting to see if there were enough piastres left to buy the *Samir* magazine and get the bus home. Once I counted wrong, got on the bus with the magazine in my hand, then turned my pocket out and found it was empty. I was seized with panic as I looked at the faces round me. Then I saw a little girl sitting by herself, and went up to her and asked her for a piastre.

* Bait Sahour is a Palestinian village not far from Jerusalem.

65

She gave it to me, and I went and sat next to her, and we laughed all the way as we looked at the adventures of Samir and Tahtah.

With the paper bag in my hand, I reached the small roundabout where the service taxis stop to let passengers off and pick others up. Standing in the middle was a traffic policeman wearing a military cap and dark glasses which reflected the people and cars in miniature, and loaded down with the number of things hanging from his belt: a stick, handcuffs, a revolver, a few hand grenades and a radio transmitter. I remembered what Umar had said about him once: was the man going straight off to the battlefield, or what? He'd considered the point and laughed. Where's the battle, my girl, he said, is the traffic in Beirut just a nuisance or is it a war? I paused, hesitating, in front of a gas station. Perhaps I should go and get the letter Salwa brought with her from Amman, a letter Shahd sent together with good things from home— *frikeh** and sage tea. This sage tea, called *miramiyyeh*, takes its name from the Virgin Mary. Hajjeh Salimeh told me the story. When the Virgin Mary fled to the mountains, she'd gather this herb and use it to wipe away the sweat on her face brought by all the running and the exhaustion. The letter; I'd better go on to Salwa's now and get it.

Salwa gave us all the news yesterday as we sat on the balcony of Su'ad's apartment. They'd managed, at last, to arrange things so they could come here. She told us about the Gulf, and the job there, and the eventual resignation. "All people seemed to look forward to over there," she

* *Frikeh* is roasted green wheat, dried, then cooked like pilau.

said, "was a pay rise and their annual leave. When I think, God help us, of all the things that went on abroad, and still do go on! And there are still Palestinians outside, too, who complain about the decision to mobilize."

"You wait," Su'ad commented. "The ones who've settled down and made a secure future for themselves will be the first to skip back to Palestine when it's liberated."

Su'ad started talking about the places she lived in after she left Jordan. "Heavens," she said, "it's a hard life, always packing up and moving on!" What she said reminded me of the way my mother used to talk about it so long ago—as if peace and quiet and settling down were just a dream. I told Su'ad and Salwa about this. "I was two years old," I said, "or three, or four. I'd never actually seen my father, because he was in prison in al-Jafr,* but I'd talk to his photograph in the morning. I'd say good morning to it. And before I went to sleep I'd blow him a kiss and say: Good night, Father. I can just remember the long wooden crates my mother would pack with jars of olives and tins of food and various papers. Usually the crates got lost and never arrived, and then she'd look sad and try and hide her tears from me. After five years they started persecuting her as well. Once the National Guard took a woman off the Jerusalem to Jericho bus because she had green eyes and long hair like my mother. They searched her and examined her identity card, and when they were sure it wasn't my mother they asked her if she was a communist too."

"Is that you, Salwa?" Umar had said, coming in and greeting her warmly. "How long have you been here?" "A

---

* Al-Jafr is in a remote part of the Jordanian desert. The prison there is mainly for political prisoners and is notorious for its harsh conditions.

week," she'd replied. "All that time," he said, "and you didn't come and see us?" He turned to me. "What's the matter with you today, Jinan? Why are you looking so miserable?" He brought a chair and sat down. "Su'ad and Jinan," he went on, smiling, "are sure to try and frighten you with stories about the civil war. Have a bit of pity on her, girls, she's only just arrived in the country." Salwa responded to his banter. "They'd started giving me instructions," she said, "about how to take cover in the doorways of buildings if the bombing started up while I was out in the street." In fact, Su'ad and I took all this very seriously, and we'd been telling Salwa how much more beautiful Beirut had been the summer before. "If only you'd been here when it was at its best, Salwa," I said. "We'd take the children off to the sea and breathe in some air for a few hours, away from all these damp houses crammed all together, and we'd stroll along the Corniche sometimes and sit in popular cafés with trees and gardens. But the way it is now, we just can't go out the way we used to do. You're lucky you've missed the battles of the last two months."

"And then there's the gardening," Umar broke in. "Just don't ask about that! They got so devoted to plants that I'd come and find them deep in discussion about *mkahhaleh* and mimosa and that carpet plant in the corner there—you'd think we had a real carpet to listen to them—and all sorts of other weird and wonderful names. When I saw how interested they suddenly were in plants, I told them they were getting old. A big interest in plants is a sign of old age, isn't that so, girls?" Su'ad and I vigorously denied this.

"And then," he went on, "there's the bird. Have you

heard about the bird? Jinan brought a songbird home for the children, and they thought about it and decided it needed a mate. So she took it to some neighbors in the Rahmeh Building, so it could be married and have some little boys and girls. And what happened? The egg hatched out a week ago and the bird became a proud father. But the neighbor won't let the family come back to us till he's taught them the nine canary languages, or so he says. Ask her if you don't believe me!" I laughed. "Yes," I said, "that's what the neighbor told me. He promised me he'd play them his tapes of birdsong and take care of them till they got big, and then give them back to us!"

I thought again of this old bird raiser. He had a houri tattooed on his right forearm and an anchor on his left, and when I asked him about them he told me he'd once been a sailor. Then he'd retired, and now he spent his days with his family, never leaving the building. "Sitting around and hearing the women talking bores me stiff," he said. "I only talk to my birds." Then he fell silent. I didn't tell the others he'd promised to give me a gardenia cutting next time I called.

Umar bustled noisily round us. "Let's make some green tea for our friend Salwa," he said. There weren't enough glasses, so we drank from children's plastic mugs. We went on with our joking. "My God," Umar said to Salwa, "if you'd only seen the girls training last summer during the mobilization." "Not me," said Su'ad, "I was pregnant with Jumana." "Well, Jinan and the others anyway," he continued, pointing at me. "If only you'd been here to see them! They used to come back from their training sessions covered with dirt and sand—we couldn't believe our eyes. And then they'd take off their uniforms and their boots, and try and show us they knew more about military things than we did." "But I wasn't very good at target practice," I said, laughing. "I couldn't focus my eyes as I took aim. How can you keep one eye open and the other one closed? I either had to have them both open or both closed." "We even suggested she should wrap a scarf over one eye," Su'ad said. "She looked just like Moshe Dayan."

We roared with laughter, from the bottom of our hearts. If Umar caught me looking serious, he'd clap his hands just in front of my face and shout out some non-sense. "We're here," he'd shout, "we're still here! The world hasn't come to an end yet!"

I reached the beginning of the alley leading to Salwa's apartment. There were old houses all bunched up against one another, then the shops selling bales of cloth, which had sprung up everywhere in the district now that the old shopping centers had closed down because of the war, and a china berry tree that flowered at the end of the summer. Then came some piles of garbage with cats dotted about on them, and finally some modern buildings at the end of the cul-de-sac. The apartment was on the top floor.

Salwa let me in, and we had a talk about the prospects of finding work for her. Then she went to her bedroom to look for the letter in her bags. There was no furniture in the place except for the sofa and the table and a few essential items piled up in boxes by the wall. I went out on to the roof, where there's a wall that turns it into a spacious balcony. The sun was very hot there, and dazzled my eyes with its glare. The roof looked out towards the distance buildings of East Beirut, where Burj Rizq and Burj Murr stand opposite one another, and on the other side you could see the tops of the buildings of Fakihani and the Cité Sportif, with their water tanks, and a jungle of intermeshed television aerials above the roof-tops. Su'ad was bound to ask me if there was any news in the letter about her own people, I thought; I must phone her when I came down. Sometimes I'd ring her up and forget what it was I wanted to say, and I'd realize that I simply wanted to talk to her; I'd talk to her about trivial things it wouldn't occur to me to mention to anyone else. She'd be sitting in the clinic in the Rahmeh Building, recording prescriptions, with Jumana in a baby's chair close by. I asked her a couple of days ago why she didn't send her back to the crèche, now that the bombing of the district was over. She'd start again at the beginning of next month, she told me.

The noise! Something extraordinary.
Suddenly,
it shrieks into the sky, whizzes around us.
Salwa comes running. Her face is pale.
I calm her. The sound barrier broken perhaps,
It's happened before.
Then,
Boom!
The earth shakes as if the building
will cave in on us. A cloud of black
smoke. The Fakihani quarter.
Coming from Fakihani. A huge mushroom.
Up it goes, and up.
Then,
Boom! Another tearing earthquake.

71

Planes.
The Israeli airforce.
Rushing footsteps on the staircase of the block,
everything confused. People, cries of
terror. The shelter. Gusts of hot air
sweep down in a series of tremors.
I've begun to think. My first thought is,
they're running.
My knees hurt. An icy shiver
from my shoulders, down my back. They're running.
They're running.
The Rahmeh Building. Yes, I saw it,
blood pouring down faces.
Down corridors, down stairs, they're running.
From the roof of the building I manage
to run. There. My body
aches with a cold shiver,
icy, I am no longer able
To move. I try to think,
but this, the Rahmeh Building,
who will escape?
I lose the faces I know.
Is it? No, perhaps no.
Feeling crushed, desperate, I remember her.
She and Jumana.

(2)

Then
all hell is loose,
a raid, four raids.
Who can . . . ?

The street was surrounded by forces of the armed struggle. Black smoke filled it, yelling filled every place, there
was the man they got out. His hair was covered with ash.

As he wailed, as he wept, he shouted: "Where's my
family?"

The bulldozer came, and the civil defense. I looked up
at her office—the clinic, on the third floor. There weren't
any floors now, and whole walls had vanished. Her house
opposite—smoke from the fire was streaming out of the
windows. The street was utterly changed. Everything
there was mixed up together. Cars were upside down,
papers whirling in the sky. Fire. And smoke. The end of
the world.

I squatted silently in a dark corner, no longer able to
move. It was chaos—the search for the dead and
injured—blood spattered on the clothes of those rescued.
Lists of names came slowly, one after the other; first the
dead, then the injured, then those who were missing. But
she, where was she, and her children? I ran to look at all
the fresh lists as they arrived, desperate to have just one of
their names. Which hospital were they in? I didn't ask
about Umar, who was sure to be out rescuing the wounded. Oh God, God! Even now it wasn't possible. Just one
name! A cold numbness crept into my hands, as if I was
paralyzed. I vowed not to leave till I found her. If she was
safe, then they were all safe.

An hour passed, or several hours, I don't remember.
Then she came through the door, and I couldn't believe
my tongue was moving and I could talk. I still don't know
how I did it.

She asked about Umar. Oddly, it hadn't struck me that Umar hadn't turned up yet. But no doubt he was busy rescuing the injured, and he'd be back in the evening to tell us about it. We asked her about the children: she'd got them out of the house, she told us. As for Umar, she'd searched till she was exhausted; something must have happened to him. No, Su'ad, we said, dear Su'ad, it's impossible, he must be with the other young men now. Somebody said he saw him during the raid, while others said they didn't see him at all. One young man who'd heard what we were saying came up and reassured me: Umar wasn't on patrol duty today, he said, so he might not be in the quarter at all.

She shuddered, then began to weep helplessly, "I asked about him everywhere," she cried, "and that's what they all said!"

Where was he then? Where was he? I didn't have the courage to believe her fears. He might come in at any moment, I thought, and he'd tell us what had happened and laugh at what he'd call our groundless fears. As she wept, I told her to try and be patient. "How much longer do I have to be patient?" she said.

I asked her again about the children, and she told me briefly that she'd left them with a friend in another quarter. "Go and be with them," I said, "and I'll wait here. I'll come and tell you when we hear something about him. Nothing's happened, of course it hasn't. Don't leave the children alone. We'll stay here, and we'll come to you the moment we have any news."

We stayed up all night, and at three in the morning there was still no news—just the monotonous din of bulldozers and the searchlights; the hospitals and the injured; martyrs we couldn't yet believe had become martyrs; families looking for lost relatives. It was impossible to take anything in under these conditions. I couldn't bring myself to believe he was injured, or . . . He was still somewhere outside the place where hands were laboring with such speed and resolution to reach the voices of the living and the bodies of the dead. And he . . . no, it was impossible.

I met him first in Jordan, in Black September, when we were in a house besieged by bedouin troops. As the bombardment grew fiercer, our fighters moved to other positions, but Shahd and I stayed with the people at the first aid post inside the house, which was at one end of Jabal Husain, on the edge of the camp. They surrounded the house all night, firing into the air and terrorizing the people crowded together in the hallway on the ground floor. Where could we go with things as they were? In the morning, we thought, they'd storm the house and arrest us; but when dawn came they withdrew for a few hours.

Im Mahmoud came and told us there was someone still asleep near the outer wall of the house, in the direction of the camp, and we ran out to him. After a few words he woke up and helped us climb the wall and jump down on the other side, and we crossed an open space within the range of the tank's guns. We were a target for snipers, and, as he urged us to make for the camp, a bombardment of howitzer artillery started up. He waved his hand to us, then went back to his ambush point near the exposed area. I met him dozens of times afterwards, but I never asked him how he'd managed to sleep when they were so close. He'd used his combat jacket as bedding, and slept with a mere wall separating them from him.

At five in the morning they came back, saying they'd found him under some rubble. Umar. Umar the Martyr. That's what they said, yet I couldn't bring myself to believe it. The martyr is dead, long live the martyr; this was no mere death, martyrs never die. Still I couldn't believe it. I had to believe it, but how could I?

The dawn stained with destruction had spoken. Umar and Umar the martyr. Why couldn't I believe it? New rays of sun seeped through the clouds of dust and spoke. Yes, it was him. I saw piles of concrete, stones, torn clothes scattered about, shattered glass, little pieces of cotton wool, fragments of metal, buildings destroyed or leaning crazily, gutted doorways, first aid workers rushing about, the surge of people around the bulldozer, the white masks of the rescuers, the wailing horns of the ambulances, the potted plants upturned, black clouds belching out from the last remaining fires, dislocated pipes. I saw the balcony that still looked out over Fakihani, and the flash of his smile as he waved goodbye yesterday. I felt torn apart by that small, unfamiliar gesture. Every day I'd just say "I'm off," and leave them up there on the balcony without actually saying goodbye. Yesterday, as Su'ad and I were standing in the doorway, I asked her, "Where's Umar?" I don't know why, but I went back to the corridor to look at him where he was still sitting on the balcony. "Bye, Umar," I said, and he waved goodbye and flashed a smile at me.

But how? With a sudden shock, the sun of the new day brought me face to face with the brutal reality. How could

I tell her? The other girls gathered round me. Let's go to her, they said.

Once, when they were living in Shatila, he was wounded in the foot by a stray bullet. I heard about it by chance, and took a bunch of lavender and went to see her, so that we could go to the hospital together. When I reached the doorway I saw her preparing food for the children. "Umar!" I cried. "Which hospital is he in? Do you know the number of the room?" She opened her mouth in amazement as I told her the news. "He didn't come back last night," she said, "but I supposed he was on duty somewhere." Confused, she quickly handed the children over to Im Hamdi and we went off to the hospital—in fact, we tried three hospitals, and didn't find him in any of them. In the end we found him lying, bandaged up, at a friend's house. He looked at us in his usual calm manner. "It's quite simple," he said. "I got treatment at the hospital and then left. I didn't want to give you any trouble. I was coming home this evening, as soon as I felt a bit more comfortable."

The other girls and I were in the car—the oppressive sun, the stagnant air, the speeding wheels. How was it possible? I tried to fight back my tears. How could we tell her? It was unbelievable. Weeping. Tears that meant he wasn't here any more. Umar, Umar the martyr—just one extra word, a word like death, yet utterly different.

I tried not to weep, I mustn't weep. But in spite of myself, I . . .

(5)

It was Fakihani, and everyone was gathered round her. The tears rolled down her cheeks. One by one, in a long line, everyone came forward to embrace her. There was no sound, except for the noise of the piles of concrete collapsing as the bulldozer pushed them about; there was nothing around us but rubble and hurrying feet and the pain of the ordeal that everyone was trying to keep under control.

I went to her apartment to find the addresses of his family in his distant country. I remembered how happy he'd been a few days before, preparing a trip to Tunisia. "Even if I can't go there," he'd said, "Su'ad can; she'll meet my mother who I haven't seen for twenty years. They'll be there for the Adha Feast* and the holiday." The children had been getting ready to travel in a plane! There'd be no plane now.

I went into the building which had been swarming with people the day before, and found it totally empty; lonely and desolate in the full light of day. The front of the Rahmeh Building was still standing opposite, but the two buildings either side of it had collapsed like a heap of biscuits. It was as if there'd been nothing, for hundreds of years, but splinters of broken furniture, stones, twisted iron rods, locks of human hair on cotton mattresses strewn here and there.

The staircase was quite empty and the door to the apartment broken. My heart beat still more painfully as my shoes crunched on the broken glass that was scattered far and wide. Windows had been wrenched from their hinges and the rubble everywhere made it look as if there'd been no home there at all the day before. Century upon century of stony dust covered, alike, things that had remained in their places and things that had been hurled

---

* The Adha is the greater of the two main Muslim feasts, coming at the end of the pilgrimage to Mecca.

aside. Ruba's bonnet lay demurely in one of the corners; there was the remains of a water-melon on the table, and the children's exercise books were still open among the stones on the floor. His room was the only place that was still in a decent state; there nothing had been smashed except the window panes. There was the small box of letters on the desk, from which voices now seemed to clamor: his family's, and Louisa's. He used to read extracts from her letters to Su'ad and myself, smiling as he skated over other pieces which he wasn't prepared to translate for us. We'd protest vigorously about this, then laugh and joke over it: we know she's a friend of yours, we said, but tell her not to dream of coming here. And Umar used to reply jokingly: "She's a good, affectionate woman. I used to talk to her a lot about you. Why are you so up in arms about her?" Then Su'ad, half joking and half serious, would come out with the popular saying: God make her happy, but keep her away from here!

His watch was still on the table, and so were the brown shells the children had brought back from the sea when he'd taken them there for the first time that summer.

My gaze became fixed on his clothes: his brown pants and beige shirt lying on the sofa, the color of flesh. Their fine texture had been transformed into something living and breathing, as if it was not just some woven material, but the wearer himself. The clothes were folded just as he himself had laid them there, ready to put on the next time. I thought of the balcony, and laughter, the way we laughed and clapped our hands at the jokes we made with one another. An upturned plate of cheese and some slices of bread had been hurled into a corner.

I couldn't look at it all any more. There was white dust

spread around inside, as if there'd been an acid fire. The empty building, the noise of pickaxes and the din from the clearing up outside—my heart was pounding and pounding as I ran back to her.

(6)

At the airport the fighters raised their hands in a military salute and fired twenty-one times into the air. Only now could he go back to the country he'd left twenty years before. Another year was about to begin, and he'd go there bearing the new name he'd chosen: Umar, Umar the martyr. He left, and with him went our laughter that rang out like silver bells. The coffin swayed above the hands that bore it, draped in the Palestinian flag, with wreaths of gorgeous roses adorning it. Had he been alive, he would have made fun of us for the black we were wearing; his smile would have flashed as he waved goodbye. Don't worry, he would have cried, I'll soon be back. If he'd been alive, he would have been laughing at what he liked to call our groundless fears.

In spite of all my efforts, I wept.

Su'ad waved goodbye to us, striving to seem like her normal self. She fought back her tears and, before reaching the departure lounge, turned and said:

"Don't worry, I'll soon be back."

Supplement

Su'ad

She would be jerked abruptly from her dream, her spine

gripped by a violent chill that shuddered through her, in her ears a voice saying: "Where are you?" For all the heat, cold sweat would be streaming from her body, and her teeth would still be chattering from the shock of the passing nightmare. She would try to piece together the fragments of the dream which had so suddenly taken possession of her, and was now goading her: Get up! Where are you?

She would try to brush it aside, as one might a big horsefly, but it would take no notice at all. Fakihani; and white dust; and patches of blood that spread and spread. White dust smothered the district, and through the gray of the smoke loomed the gutted shells of blocks and the debris of houses razed to the earth. Stretched out on the ground was the body of a man she didn't know, cloaked in blood. The time was maybe a month before the raid, or just a few days before.

Su'ad told Jinan afterwards that she actually saw the man who'd appeared in her dream, lying covered in his own blood, near Umar in the hospital. There were piles of bodies lying stiff and frozen in the cold store of the hospital morgue. She was able to recognize Umar from his military shoes. He was lying on his stomach, and when she approached him she saw that other man; the man of the dream. And the white dust of Fakihani.

Umar leaving

Su'ad was weeping. "He was lying there asleep," she said, "like an angel. What were you thinking of, my love, before you fell asleep?" She intoned the words as though she were singing, and the music of her voice infused the surrounding darkness, sweetly and delicately. Her voice grew softer, till what she said could no longer be heard; then, suddenly, it swelled up again. "How handsome you looked in that suit, my love, that morning when I left Jumana fast asleep and went off to Sabra. I tired myself out carrying the heavy bags full of the groceries we needed. I found him in the house, ready to set off. He put his belt on over his jacket, and joked with me. 'Here you are, Su'ad,' he said, 'I'm putting my belt on over my suit, the way you like it.' He told me I shouldn't be carrying all those bags, that I'd get tired. I said it was all right. 'Well,' he said, 'you'll be traveling in a few days, and you'll have a rest when you arrive.' I asked him if he wasn't going to the hospital for his blood test. 'We're on alert today,' he said. 'I'm going on patrol first.' Jumana cried and clung on to him as he left, and I was filled with a sense of premonition. I took her away from him, and never saw him again except at the hospital."

Jinan

I felt I must see him, to bid him farewell as a friend should; "I'll come with you," I said to Dr. Yusuf. The red lights of the ambulance weren't flashing, and there was a stench coming from the yellowish, bloodstained sheet on the stretcher.

The ambulance left our blacked-out quarter, left behind the noise of bulldozers droning monotonously beneath the yellow searchlights that played on the buildings of Fakihani. It was in the doorway, the doorway of the Fakihani building, that they'd found him among the ashes and rubble. The last young man to see him alive said he was rescuing civilians still inside the building when he was hit, perhaps in the third of the air raids. He was going back to get the last people out through the thick black smoke. In the doorway it was . . .

We drove on through Beirut, amid scenes of what I suppose is called normal life—crowded streets and the colored lights of the shop windows and the seething traffic in Hamra Street. The ambulance came to a halt behind some vehicles unable to move because of the people pouring out of one of the cinemas. We reached the University Hospital road junction. There was the stench, the same stench; and outside the thing called normal life.

As the door of the hospital morgue opened, the thick, congealed stench flew out suddenly into my face. He was lying there in his combat gear, looking peaceful and calm, the only outward signs of injury a few bruises on his head, and some lines of dried blood on his face—which had not, I swear, lost the expression, or the smile, that I knew. I gazed first at him, then at his olive-green suit, and at his belt. There was some dust on the toe cap of the black military boot. As I looked at him, and at his unchanging expression, he was silent, and yet it was as though he was talking to me. How did it happen, Umar? How could a few wounds and bruises bring you to this? His face had been slightly altered by the traces of a blow and the effects of the rubble; but the old expression was there, full of wisdom and irony.

There was stench all around me; I held my breath for as long as I could, then smelt it again. The same stench as on that Black September, covering the seven hills of Amman. I nearly fainted once in the Jabal Husain camp. As dizziness and nausea gripped me, I pulled myself

83

together, and went to the door to fill my lungs with the fresh air of the world outside; it was sunset, and, for all the disasters and the bombardment from the heavy artillery, the air remained deeply pure and invigorating. Then I managed to return to my work amid the stagnant atmosphere, and the yellow candle-light flickering on the surgical scissors and needle, and the wounds like gaping mouths. Things won't always be like this, I thought, there's still some fresh air left in the world.

Karim was there too, Dr. Yusuf told me, and Abu Antun. And . . . The stench was all round me still. As I left, sheets stained with great patches of blood were being placed over the empty stretcher for the injured.

*   *   *   *

I remember that the sea had a stench in Beirut. It blew whenever the horizon exploded out of the lovely expanse of blue. After the war there were barriers of sheet metal,* but they didn't keep the stench out.

The sidewalk on the Corniche was thronged with traders selling roasted corn, peanuts and lupin beans, but the stench didn't disappear.

Displays of cheap, gaudy clothes sprang up everywhere on the tin-built stalls, and traders began to throng in from Souk Sursock. But the stench didn't disappear.

Yet the smell of the sea came suddenly to an end, blending with the black tar and the smell of rotten food, with a smell of human bodies.

---

* The reference here is to the countless small makeshift shops erected after the war. The sheet metal from which whole rows of these shops were made would give the effect of a "barrier."

The sea. No; it was the same stench, but it reminded you of the smell of the sea.

The sea had a smell that was like the man you love: beads of sweat and lemon flowers and the onset of a rosy twilight.

The sea began to take on the smell of a speeding ambulance with its wailing siren and its red lights flashing on and off. It was the same smell. I breathed it in, and I wasn't afraid.

The Canary
and the Sea

The sea is the deep-seated land of our call.
The sea is our portrait.
Who has no land
Has no sea.
　(Mahmoud Darwish, *In Praise of the Tall Shadow*)

I

(1)

My name is Abu Husain al-Shuwaiki. I'm a child of Shuwaika, yet I've only been there twice in my life, once in 1963 when it was full of people, and once in 1970 when most of the people had either been taken off to prison or gone away in search of work. Shuwaika, let me tell you, is a small village to the north of Tulkarm, near a mountain they call the Cape. You can still see there the fortifications and gun sites set up by the Iraqi army during that war which attempted to liberate us from the Zionists in 1948.

Shuwaika, my home village, is an expanse of green at the end of a mountain range, with lemon and orange groves and silver sunbeams on the olive leaves, and if you stand on the roof of our house you can see the sea and the Natanya district—alas for Natanya, which I can no longer visit, and the sea stretching out to the far horizon! But, you may ask, isn't Shuwaika still Shuwaika, even though they took it in 1967? What is there left that they haven't taken? Before 1967 it was a border village, and the trees, which were right on the frontier itself, were each divided into two halves. One half belonged to the people of the village and the Israelis picked the fruit on the other side.

People standing near the frontier on our side were forbidden to look over onto the other; and if anyone so much as stretched out their hand or put it over the border, they were killed straightaway by the Israelis. They used to place white flags on the open ground near the edge of the orchard, and there were whitewashed stones dotted about there. If you don't like white, I share your feelings; I can't stand the color. All night great searchlights would light up the border—the trees, I mean, I'm sorry—and the land round about, to stop anyone trying to cross over to the other side.

(2)

I visited Shuwaika after the 1967 occupation, but didn't cross, even though this was no longer difficult. Instead I went to Acre to call on my mother's brother, who'd originally got separated from his mother—my grandmother—at Tulkarm bus station, in the rush and chaos of the Exodus. You know what it was like: the bullets and the explosions, and people running around in panic—although war was child's play in those days compared to now. My grandmother was frightened and didn't realize he was missing till she'd got on the bus to Amman. It turned out that he'd thought she was on the bus to Acre, and had hung on to the rear ladder of that bus till it reached its destination. There he'd wandered the streets until an old lady in Acre, who had no husband or children, had taken him in and brought him up. When my grandmother made enquiries about him over the radio, he heard his name and sent a radio message back, and she managed to arrange a meeting with him with the aid of the Red Cross. When she saw him at the Mandelbaum Gate in Jerusalem she didn't recognize him, and he didn't recognize her; he'd been eleven years old when he left her, and now he was twenty-two. She'd start asking what had happened to So-and-So, and he'd reply by asking what had happened to Such-and-Such; Where's Mahmoud now, she'd ask, and he'd say, Where's Rayhana now? They finally ended up just standing facing one another and asking questions. They were, of course, standing, separated, on the two sides of the line.

My uncle in Acre was working on a lorry that transported vegetables, and he took me with him on his trips. I saw the walls of Acre and the old cannons dating from the time of al-Jazzar* and the one gate of Acre (apart from

---

* Ahmad al-Jazzar was governor of Acre, at the end of the eighteenth and beginning of the nineteenth century.

the one the Israelis tried to build outside the walls, plac-
ing a monument to the spy, Cohen, nearby). I saw so
many things! I went to Haifa, and climbed Mount Carmel, and saw Lake Tiberias, and Tel Aviv, and Nahariya,
and the district of Sukhna. I saw Palestine—then my
permit expired, and they flatly refused to renew it. I
remembered my grandmother who'd died in exile and
seen her lost son just once, behind the frontier line.

(3)

After the 1948 Exodus we lived in Lebanon; in fact my
father's mother was Lebanese, from a Ras Beirut* family.
My grandfather met her in a strange way. The Turkish
army had taken her brother to Palestine for compulsory
military service, and my great-grandmother, deeply wor-
ried about her son, went there to look for him and took
her three daughters with her. In the course of her rigor-
ous journey she had to leave her daughters with some
bedouins who were camping in Northern Palestine.
"Look after these girls for me till I come back," she said,
"and God save you." They agreed, and the girls settled
down with them while she went off on her search. Now
my grandfather was a camel trader, who went among the
bedouin to rest himself and his camels before continuing
on his way, and he happened to see the girls as he passed
by. Being very much taken with them, he came to a quick
decision and said to them: "Come on, let's go"—just like
that, without so much as a by your leave. The girls didn't
know what to do, but the firm tone of command in his

* Ras Beirut is a prosperous part of West Beirut bordering on the sea. The American
University of Beirut is sited there.

voice made them obey at once. As a result a marriage contract was drawn up for my grandmother, his brother married another sister and his cousin married the third.

Fifty years later I proposed to a Lebanese girl, but was turned down by her family because I was a Palestinian and a foreigner. Then, when her grandmother discovered a distant relationship with my own, they changed their mind and agreed to accept me.

(4)

In the middle of the sixth month of the year Israel invaded Lebanon, I was posted to the southern area of Beirut—Borj al-Barajneh, the Sullam district, Mraijeh and the sands of Shuwaifat. I took over the last Shuwaifat line that extended to Khalda; I had twenty comrades with me, and we were on the front line, in direct contact with the Israeli forces.

It was ten o'clock in the morning, and I wanted to change my team; this would be changed over every three days, with ten men being replaced by ten others. I set off with the company, and we went through the Sullam district, then through the sands of Shuwaifat, till we reached the town of Shuwaifat, on the edge of which we'd established a position. Just as we arrived, we were surprised by a violent artillery assault on our line. The Israeli forces were trying to advance on three fronts, Khalda-Shuwaifat, Dair Qubil-Shuwaifat and Kfarshima-Shuwaifat. I told my comrades to lie flat on the ground and stay there. The bombardment went on for about a quarter of an hour, then suddenly we heard the din of Israeli armed vehicles and advancing infantry. We engaged with them on the Khalda-Shuwaifat line and destroyed two tanks. On the second line the Israelis met with some difficulties; they attempted to force their way through with a bulldozer, but were thwarted by our fire. On the third line a company from the Lebanese Communist Party destroyed three tanks. They renewed their advance on our line, and we put two more tanks out of action. The battle continued, and we saw their infantry flee, retreating whenever we hit the tanks. At four o'clock one of our comrades in the joint forces advanced on a tank and tossed in a couple of hand grenades, and the tank behind it sprayed 500-pounders at him from its powerful gun and killed him. The Israeli forces succeeded in occupying the territory we'd been on, and we retreated to fresh fighting positions in al-Tayru and the sands of Shuwaifat.

(5)

The Americans who landed in Lebanon in 1958 had their camp in the middle of al-Tayru and the sands of Shuwaifat. I was just a boy at the time and went to have a look at them. The first time I saw them I was standing in a field of lettuce that belonged to Elias Thabit. Their regiments passed me heading for the camp, and whenever a soldier went by I'd call out: "May God curse your father!" A black American soldier came up to me and tweaked my ear with a grin. "Hush," he said. "Some of the soldiers are Arabs. If they tell the others what you're saying, they'll beat you up."

They didn't beat me up, or pay the slightest attention to me. Afterwards, at the request of the Young Nationalists,

I began going to the camp with other youngsters, to rifle what we could there. We'd go in on the pretext of selling chicklets chewing gum and wander about the camps pilfering arms and clothes; then we'd slip away via the camp that lay in an area surrounded by orchards and lupini fields and sugar cane growing alongside the irrigation channels. Once we got hold of a Bren gun, and at other times we got military uniforms, army drinking cups and hand grenades.

My eyes were opened to new things. I saw the Lebanese Air Force, supported by the Americans, making strikes on the mountain, and I heard about Jumblat and Chamoun and the Phalangists. I saw Americans, during their training, parachuting in the High Dunes— Ghazzar district. They used to cover the ground with the fabric of their parachutes, and they'd be tied to strings like plucked chickens. The other lads and I would run up to them and hit them with stones which we'd throw or fire from catapults.

(6)

We lived in Sunaubara in Ras Beirut, and I soon came to feel that the word Palestinian had a different meaning in Lebanon, conjuring up, immediately, the army, authority and the secret police. I had relatives living in temporary tents in the camps, and the police would come and say; "Move those away from here." Then a dozen men from the area would work together to take up every tent and move it to a spot specified by the police. The tent poles would be fixed on to wooden planks parallel with the ground, so that they could be lifted up and moved elsewhere whenever the police felt like ordering it. Prison lay in wait for anyone who dared attach tinplating to the roof of a tent, or hammered nails in the wooden tent poles. And if a woman spilt water outside the tent, she was liable to a fine of 25 Lebanese pounds; for how could a woman, any woman, be permitted to soil the fair, verdant face of Lebanon by spilling filthy washing water on it?

(7)

In 1972 I was working as shop foreman in a factory for making wooden furniture in East Beirut. The owner of the factory was a decent man, but he had a brother in the Phalangist Party. There were three or four of us Palestinians working for him, and after May 1973 he came to resent us and made it clear our presence there was an embarrassment to him. "You're refugees," he'd say, "and yet you try and tell us how to do things. This is our country. You shouldn't be here at all." We argued with him, and finally lost our tempers and left. I didn't care, because our wages were always less than other peoples'. They always used to call us "the Palestinians," and the way they said it had a special ring that upset me. "Look, my friend," I said, "you're Lebanese. Do you hear me say 'the Lebanese' all the time, and in that tone of voice?"

(8)

When the 1973 clashes began I naturally took part, and we all enlisted when the fighting grew fiercer, feeling that the Palestinians in Lebanon were in danger. I went to Borj al-Barajneh camp. There were only two or three rifles in the office there, plus a Kalashnikov and two Simonovs, and large numbers of young men took turns using them. We organized continuous patrols of the camp.

After 1973 the police posts were withdrawn from the camp, and people rejoiced and praised God from the bottom of their hearts. I'd walk round the tracks of the camp and meet friends with enormous grins on their faces. The police had gone! The police, the secret police had gone—pursued by a million curses! How we celebrated their departure!

(9)

I started off with a group of militiamen, and in 1974 I was placed in charge of a group of seven or eight men, which doubled its numbers over the next six months. In 1975 I went abroad for military training, and in 1976 I returned to the busy souks of Beirut.

The city center was very beautiful before the war: there were souks, shops, people buying and selling, people working and producing things; the bustle never stopped day or night. After the war it became deserted and rather ugly. The loveliest city in the world becomes unbearable when it's deserted; finally it had been the people, the Beirutis, who'd made it so beautiful. There'd be clashes in the center of the city, and the enemy would flee; they were lightly armed, as we were, but the quality of courage was greater among our people. We'd taunt them and curse them, with only a wall separating us. For them the clashes sprang from a desire to dominate, for us it spelt defense of our very existence. You'll remember April, and the slaughter in the bus:* it was innocent civilians who were killed. It was the enemy, of course, who initiated and caused it. I became responsible for a squadron in the souks, in the heart of Beirut.

The Nimjeh Square really is "The Square of the Star,"† for it's right in the center, with roads leading off from it to all parts of Beirut. Around it are the Lebanese Parliament, the banks and the souks. From the souks you reach the Borj Square, which is also called the Place des Martyrs, and from there you go down to the Port quarter, and you've reached the sea. In the end it was the Place des Martyrs which separated them from us, with them on one side, in the souks, and us on the other; this square, formerly the focus of the largest and most important district in Beirut, had become the sole barrier between us. There were cheap hotels around the square, and stations for communal taxis going to all parts of Lebanon, markets for fruit and vegetables, the Nouriyya souk, and row upon row of shops. You opened one eye and closed the other, and there was Souk Sursock in front of you, with all its winding paths and narrow entrances. And on the other side there was the Rivoli cinema and the women of Mutanabbi Street. All the din and bustle of Beirut was to be found there. Then, when the war came, so many things stopped in an instant. There was no longer the deafening noise, and there were no crowds any more; just the subdued shuffling of stealthy feet. The skeletons of

* The reference is to an incident on April 13, 1975, when a bus full of Palestinians traveling from Tal al-Zaatar to Beirut was stopped and sprayed with bullets by Phalangists as it passed through the Christian village of Ain al-Rummaneh. It was this incident which triggered the fighting between the Palestinians and the Phalangists.
† *Nijmeh* means "star" in Palestinian Arabic dialect. The classical Arabic form of the word is *najmah*.

old, blackened buildings still testify to their former beauty, and dark green wild grass sprouts from the gaps in the barricades of sandbags; it climbs up the walls, too, and spreads everywhere, flourishing as it likes in the empty streets. All that separates us in the Borj square is the statue of the martyrs on their stone pedestal. They hold out their hands and open their strangled mouths, but make no sound.

(10)

We learned from our experience during the civil war: how to cross streets, and move around, and establish fortifications; what cul de sacs were favorable for fighting; how to move from place to place during a shelling; what streets exposed us to sniping; how to make vests that would protect us against the sniper's bullet and so allow us to be mobile. We'd fight with whatever we had, trying out various tactics to test the strength of the forces defending a particular building: what was the enemy's range, and how many men were there? Then we'd get to work with the rocket-propelled grenades or automatic weapons, or whatever we had available, advance towards the building and occupy the ground floor. After that we'd start to take over each floor in turn using ropes and hooks and long ladders, and because we were *fida'iyin** we were able to take over a whole building with seven or eight men. To our surprise the Phalangists would abandon the building and leave it to us. They relied, basically, on sniping and artillery bombardment.

* As noted earlier, the general meaning of *fida'iyin* is "those ready to sacrifice their lives for their country." Here it has the more specific implication of "Palestinian Commandos."

At the end of 1976 we withdrew from the Commercial Quarter, being replaced there by the Arab Deterrent Force, and moved on to Fakihani.

In 1978, during the Israeli attack on the South, I was in Tyre right on the front line, close to the Zionists in the Borj al-Shamali camp. The Israelis bombarded from the air and on the ground, trying to advance from a number of positions, but failed to achieve their goal because they'd opened up a single broad front.

When that war was over, I returned to Fakihani and went on with my work in the squadron dealing with the recruitment and mobilization of the militia. Then, in 1981, my unit was sent back to the Commercial Quarter.

On July 17, 1981 we were in al-Azariyya, and I had with me a young Frenchman called François, who was one of the best of our combatants. That day he woke me up and said: "I'm going to Fakihani to get a pair of field glasses from Umar."

He set off in the navy blue tracksuit which he loved to wear, accompanied by his friend Sirhan, who never left his side even during military operations. The three of them—Sirhan, Umar and François—were in the Rahmeh Building when the Israeli air force made its first strike, but were unharmed, and moved to the entrance of the building.

In the second strike a thousand pound bomb hit the skylight, and they were killed, together with our comrade Yahya and the guard posted at the entrance.

As it grew later, with our comrade François still not returned, we were setting up defenses in the Place des Martyrs, opposite the Phalangists. The sky was thick with planes, and I went on to the roof of the building to get a better look. There was smoke rising, and I could wait no longer; I went down to Riad al-Solh Square and questioned those who were there. One of them told me there'd been air strikes in the district around the Arab University.

I took a jeep and went there at once. Just by the gas station the road was blocked, and everything was in chaos, with women and children and old people rushing around the streets. I was very upset at first, because they were preventing us from getting the car into the quarter. Then we got out, and ran and ran till we reached the city stadium.

I looked out on Fakihini. It was as though I'd been away for ten years. There were cars overturned, stones, people carrying bodies, ambulances—I no longer recognized the district.

I spent two weeks in Fakihani, working day and night to help clear the rubble and search for bodies. For the whole fortnight no morsel of food passed my lips—just water or a glass of juice when I felt I needed it, from a trader near the stadium.

There was no longer any room for bodies in the hospital morgue, and at the Barbir hospital they put François and Sirhan in the same drawer, on the same stretcher; each had his head placed to one side and his body cradled in the embrace of his comrade. So François, the stranger who'd become one of us, found a companion to stay by his side in death, and young Sirhan clung to his friend to the end.

They found Umar at the entrance, covered with broken glass and rubble.

Abu Antun heard people screaming during the raid and ran back, leaving his wife and children not far from Abu Abdu's vegetable stall. He'd promised to take his wife out that day and take her to call on some relations. Then a piece of shrapnel pierced his heart, and there was an end to the picnic together, and to their whole life together. Abu Abdu was killed too, with his vegetables hurled in all directions around him.

When we found Abu al-Ghadhab nine days later, he was still seated on a chair in the finance office. He'd been squashed flat, but we identified him from the color of his shirt and the identity card in his pocket.

It was twelve days before we managed to locate my dear friend Shawqi. He was completely shriveled up, like a piece of dried fish, and I recognized him from his pajamas. He'd been asleep, and, as the position of his body showed me, was just preparing to get up. His wife wasn't killed, because she was hanging out washing on the balcony. The first shell fell directly on her house, and it was a vacuum bomb, which sucked out the air from the room where her husband and two children were, causing it to collapse. The part where she was flew up, then fell in a single piece, and she found herself hanging to some electric wiring. She threw herself down into the street, and began to run frantically in the direction of the Arab University.

We kept on searching for bodies, following the scent like tracker dogs; we'd dig and dig till we nosed out a new body among the victims.

II

(1)

The enemy were reaching out towards Shuwaifat, trying,

now, to gain control of the airport. They'd demand a ceasefire after each battle, then take the opportunity of improving their positions, using their bulldozers to set up new strongholds.

On the last Friday in June I pushed on, with a group of comrades, to forward positions near the Pepsi Cola factory in Shuwaifat. I selected a spot to dig ourselves in, and the group took up its positions opposite the enemy.

At five in the morning on Sunday August 1, 1982 an Israeli reconnaissance detachment advanced to a point between the eastern runway and the Sullam Quarter, moving into a side street ten yards from our forward group, within range of our fire. We fired into them, and they fled towards the Pepsi Cola factory, leaving sixteen dead behind them.

At 5:30 their infantry and armed vehicles advanced towards us, accompanied by Phalangist forces. Their reconnaissance detachment was part civilian and part military, and there was something like a squadron of tanks and another of infantry on a front of 250 yards. We were placed opposite them, and clashes went on till the following day.

We had a comrade from the Lebanese Communist Party, who leaped into the middle of the road and fired at the first tank in the column. As he prepared to set off, I called to him to keep under cover, but he didn't wait, standing in the middle of the road and tossing in a hand grenade. There was an explosion of fire inside it. Then the tank behind fired a 500-pounder at him and the grenades on his back exploded. His head flew off, but the headless body walked on for another five or six paces before falling to the ground.

They'd fire whatever they had in the way of shells and cluster bombs and shatter bombs, which exploded in the air and wrought havoc on the ground. They used howitzers and incendiary phosphorus bombs and all kinds of bombs that are prohibited under international law.

They advanced only 150 yards in a full twelve hours, even though our front comprised a mere twenty-five fighters of mixed forces. The Israeli attack was halted under our fire, and they began to fire at us with their tanks. I saw some of them throw their rifles on to their backs and slip away, and we took advantage of their flight to shoot at them with our small arms and mortar bombs.

Twelve tanks and a personnel carrier were destroyed in the battle, along with three bulldozers. There were also a large number of dead and wounded in their ranks.

On that Sunday, the first of August, they occupied Beirut Airport by means of a trick. A group of their commandos got in under artillery cover in vehicles belonging to the Lebanese army and police, and hand-to-hand clashes went on in the main airport building from nine in the morning right through till evening. They dropped 200,000 bombs on Beirut that day, but in spite of that they were only able to get into the airport after a ferocious battle with the Palestinians and their allies.

(2)

I left the Sullam Quarter on the morning of August 2, during a ceasefire which would, I knew, be so short that it would be over before it began. My wife and five children were in Saqiyat al-Janzir, and I'd look in on them every few days and make sure they had bread and other food. I

wanted to take some food there, but couldn't find anything. Then, by chance, I found someone selling melons
and bought four to take with me. "What is there to eat?" I
asked Im Husain. "God, we've got nothing," she said.
"Whatever you've brought will be fine." "Here are some
melons," I said. "Make do with them for the moment. I
couldn't find any bread. I'll go out and see if I can find
some."

I put out food for some birds I had—some canaries. I
loved canaries, and I had twenty-five of them, which I'd
evacuated, along with the family, to Saqiyat al-Janzir.
They were kept in our home in Fakihani till it was hit, in a
huge cage which I'd made for them on the balcony, three
feet by six. I liked to smoke a *nargila* sometimes and listen
to them twittering—just imagine, you could hear them
twittering right in the middle of Fakihani! If you heard a
canary there, you'd know the sound was coming from our
apartment, which was opposite the Rahmeh Building,
right above Abu Ali the shopkeeper, if you know him.

When I went to give the canaries some cannabis seeds,
I found one of them dead—there'd been no food for them
in the cage before I got there. He was one of those lovely
birds that chirp and sing a lot, yellow with a touch of light
orange. I was very upset, and, to be frank, felt from that
moment on that something was going to happen to me.
"Why did you leave him without any food?" I said to Im
Husain. "How could you do a thing like that?" "We were
in the shelter," she said. "There was an air raid, and we
were hiding down below."

Right through the war I'd had no sensation of death,
and I'd laugh and joke with the other fighters. The shelling was constant and battles never ceased, yet we'd fry

eggs and pick figs and grapes whenever we had a moment's rest. I felt comfortable, and would move about during the air raid; even when the car I went around in was hit a number of times by shrapnel, I took no notice of it. I had, as I said, no sense of impending death. My comrades told me several times to take care, and even Nasir Atris would come over to me every day and say: "Don't get yourself killed, Abu Husain. Be careful." I certainly didn't want to die, but just imagine—he'd come by every day and say the same thing! He fell in battle finally, after I myself had been wounded.

From my home I went to the Hreik Quarter, where I met our comrade Nabil al-Sahli who was with us in the combat squadron in Sullam. "Nabil," I said, "we need some bread at home, and we can't find any anywhere." "I know the lads of the Liberation Army," he said. "Let me go and see them. If they've got any bread, I'll send it to Im Husain." He got in his car and drove off, and was killed the very same day I was hit, by the same Israeli ambush in the Sullam Quarter that had wounded me earlier.

I returned to the Hreik office and went upstairs to inspect the follow-up detachment that was resting before going into battle. There was heavy shelling at the time, and I suddenly caught sight of myself in the mirror fixed up in the entrance and saw how my beard had grown. "Well," I said to myself, "if something happens and I get killed, at least I can die looking good!" I borrowed a razor from the young men and shaved myself with it, striving to fight a sense that all wasn't well with me. I felt pensive and tired and anxious, and I sensed that day that death was abroad. I applied some eau de cologne and was just going out of the door to set off when a radio message came saying that I should head for the Sullam Quarter. The Israeli forces were trying to enter Sullam, moving towards the quarter from the area around the Faculty of Science at the Lebanese University. The message said that the combined forces had repelled the assault and that the Israelis hadn't yet entered Sullam. I was to go there at once.

(3)

Our squadron's front line stretched from the airport to the edge of Sullam, and the Israelis were now concentrating their pressure here, because, if they broke through, they'd be able to reach Cocody Hill, overlooking the Shatila-airport roundabout and the Borj al-Barajneh Camp.

My task was to enter Sullam in any way I could, since I was the commander of the squadron, which was composed of three armed detachments, and comprised twenty-five fighters of the Palestinian Resistance and the Lebanese National Movement.

As I moved off, shells were falling like rain on the Hreik Quarter and the surrounding district. It was a random, indescribable bombardment, of shatter bombs that exploded in the air before raining death and destruction down on to the ground, together with mortars and howitzers and cluster bombs. The only things they didn't use against us were nuclear weapons.

After I'd walked about two and a half miles, I reached the beginning of Mraijeh, where there'd been an Amal road block. I looked round carefully, but saw no sign of it; the street was absolutely deserted. "Something must have

happened," I thought. Then a landrover came out of
Sullam. In it was our comrade Sharbal from the combined forces of the Lebanese Communist Party, who told
me the Israelis were about 150 yards from their office at
the main entrance to Sullam. I asked him if he'd seen
them. He hadn't seen them, he said, but of course he'd
been able to hear the noise of their equipment and soldiers. Then a car came up with two young men from the
news agency, WAFA. They'd heard the Israelis shout out,
"Surrender, you terrorists," through a loud-hailer, but
hadn't been able to identify the point on which the Israelis
had been concentrating.

I got into the car with them, and returned to the
headquarters of the combined forces in the Hreik Quarter to tell them the Israelis had entered Sullam and were
approaching the al-Tahwita district. "That's crazy,"
someone said. "There's nothing there."

All radio communication with Sullam had been cut off.
I went out again and returned there on foot, at a run. I
had to get back in there at all costs.

As I reached the edge of al-Tahwita I met four men
from the combined forces, who had a Volkswagen mini-
van. One of them, called Ibrahim, had been a comrade of
mine in earlier battles, and was now a second lieutenant
with Fatah. "What's happening?" I asked him, "we want
to get to Sullam." "So do I," he said, "but I'm waiting till
the bombardment eases up a bit." I said that we could go
in together, and he agreed.

We waited for a while, and the bombardment eased up
about 12.30. "Come on," I said, "let's start. Shall we
walk? Let's walk." But we took the car, and one of the
lads got in and sat next to Ibrahim on the front seat.

"What?" Ibrahim said. "We've got Abu Husain with us, and you want to sit here? Get in the back."

I'd known Ibrahim since the two year war, and now here he was with me in Sullam. It was strange how we kept meeting up with one another in different places.

The vehicle was white, and was like an ambulance. I sat beside Ibrahim and the four young men were in the back. When we'd reached the edge of Mraijeh and were about 300 yards from Sullam, it occurred to me that the car was going extremely slowly. "What's the problem?" I asked Ibrahim. He said it had taken a knock in the front and the balance of the wheels had been affected.

As we talked, we drove by the church that stands on the edge of Sullam, and I saw three shelled vehicles that hadn't been there that morning. "Shall we get out and walk?" I said. "It's quicker by car, Abu Husain," he said. "Let's get to Sullam, and then get out and walk."

After reaching the edge of Sullam, we intended to cross a further road junction, then get out. But just as we'd reached the junction, I suddenly saw them on the left—a tank and about twenty Israeli soldiers standing there.

"Look out, lads," I shouted. "The Israelis! The Jews!"

We all reached for our guns. There was no possible chance for us to go back; our only option was to carry on and try and finish our journey.

The soldiers immediately pointed their rifles towards the car and opened fire on us, and our men took their weapons and returned the fire. I took out my pistol, raised it and fired twice, with my right hand. Then I looked down to examine the pistol, but couldn't see it. Blood was streaming onto my face; I'd taken a bullet in the head, and two in the left hand, and felt that both my legs had been hit. It all seemed really quite simple, as if I'd just been pricked by a needle; all I felt otherwise was the blood pouring on to my face and blinding my eyes. Everything seemed to stop—it was all happening in a few moments. They were firing ceaselessly at the car, and I heard the noise of bullets raining, showering down, all round me. Pss... Pss... Ss... Ss. It was like huge hailstones dropping down on to the hot metal of the car we were in—a succession of small sounds, sharp, cold and muffled.

I stretched out to retrieve my pistol, and shot from behind Ibrahim's back, as he leaned forward over the steering wheel in his efforts to increase speed. They were ten yards away from us now. The car had begun to move slower, then slower still; all the tires had been punctured. I opened the door with my right hand, which was still untouched, and threw myself out before the car stopped, feeling it was all over, that there was no way out now. My only thought was to avoid the bullets and the enemy in front of me.

I heard the shouts and groans of the men. I don't want to remember that scene, which tears my heart even now. There were five of them, all young men—the oldest was barely twenty-six. As I threw myself out, I said that everything was over, it was all over, and I felt I was dying. I recited the *shahadah.**

* This is a fundamental Muslim formula: "I witness that there is no God but God, and I witness that Muhammad is His Prophet." It is recited on all major occasions, and would naturally be recited by a Muslim who feels he or she is about to die.

There was a wall, and when I threw myself from the car my face struck it. As my body struck the wall in its turn, it was tossed and fell so that it finally faced them, my back being against the wall with the elbow above my wounded left hand on the ground. My legs were stretched out, and my head back against the wall. There they were in front of me, before my eyes. I couldn't see the car any more; all I could see, all I could focus on, was them. I looked up, expecting to see them swivel the tank's gun which was aimed at the car and turn its fire on me. I saw the infantry soldiers too, with their rifles fixed to their waists. I watched them, and waited.

As I gazed at the tank, I saw the man in charge of its gun turn it in my direction and open fire. At that moment I felt as though I was flying through the air, spinning through space. They hit me and wounded my hand, but I didn't know exactly where I'd been hit; I was flying, hovering in the air. I was conscious of the bullets reaching me, of one striking me and the rest exploding behind my head, around my head, above my head, hitting the wall. I sank to the ground, barely conscious, aware only of the shells passing over me. Fragments rained down on me like sparks from a fire. Bullets hit the dirt sidewalks or the asphalt or the wall, missed me in spite of the close range, or perhaps because I was just too close for the range of the tank's gun.

I felt my senses fading, and before I lost consciousness I had a vision of my five children in front of me, three girls and two boys. How would they live after I was dead? What would become of them? My baby girl was twenty days old, and I'd named her after my mother. I saw her now, kicking her legs in front of me, they were all there before my eyes. She was just a baby, and I'd only seen her twice. I still had no clear idea of how she looked.

I lost consciousness, and while unconscious I had another vision. I saw low hills, then a mountain, then a river with a long dusty road by the side of it, lined with trees. The whole scene appeared to me. There, facing me, was a group of people sitting beneath a huge tree, singing and clapping their hands. Their heads seemed real, but their bodies were shadows. I walked up to them.

I saw Abu Antun, Umar, Abu al-Ghadab, Yahya and all the martyrs from the Rahmeh Building in Fakihani. They were sitting in a circle and singing. Shawqi, my closest friend, looked round and saw me. Then he got up and ran towards me with open arms, crying at the top of his voice: "Abu Husain!" His voice made an eerie echo. "You've come at last, dear friend," he cried. "Welcome, welcome!" He approached to embrace me, and I woke.

I woke with my face to the ground and my wounded right hand beneath my chest. I opened my eyes, but they were turned to the wall, not towards them. I was lying flat. Then I saw the watch on my wrist, and began to ask myself: "Am I alive or dead?"

There was no agonizing pain; I simply felt as though my body was some lump tossed to the ground, and I couldn't move. I felt absolutely no fear, but there flashed into my mind the memory of a young man who'd gone up to his apartment in the Hreik Quarter to change his clothes. We were in the entrance of the building, and advised him not to go up during the frantic shelling, but he insisted. Then the bombardment grew fiercer still, and shells fired in from the sea demolished the walls and doors of the entrance, bringing them down around us. We heard him scream out "Help, yamma!" He'd been standing in his living room when a huge piece of shrapnel suddenly came and tore off half his leg, sliced it off like a knife. We ran up to the fourth floor, where we found him crawling towards the door of the apartment, and dragged him painfully down, but couldn't get him out to the street. I squeezed the artery tight. "Don't be afraid," I said, "just go to sleep. When the shelling eases off, we'll get you out of here straightaway." I laid him out on a foam mattress, and he said: "Send my love to my mother, and my brothers and sisters."

He was shaking, and had turned very pale. The tears flowed down my face as he spoke to me. Half an hour later we managed to get him to hospital, and gave him some blood, but he died ten minutes later. There he was, a Palestinian lad, eighteen years old, whose family were in the shelter of another building and who'd just come home to change his pants.

I felt no pain. I still wasn't completely conscious, and would pass out, then come to again. I'd hear a voice from time to time, or a roar, as my eardrums were blasted by violent explosions nearby. There'd be small pieces of black, powdery shrapnel, like thorns, then I'd hear nothing clearly. I won't move, I thought, because *they* are near me. I'll stay and sleep here till nightfall, then I'll crawl out of the area. I hung on. I hung on for several hours, from half past twelve. It was four hours perhaps; I was too exhausted to be capable of taking note of the time, and it wasn't important in any case. Then I heard a roar. They were switching off the engine of the tank and starting it up again. They were still there.

I lay without moving, totally still. The blood pouring from my head was clotting round my mouth and nose and making breathing difficult, but I held on, forcing my breath in and out. Specks of blood would be expelled with my breath because I was breathing so hard, but I tried to stay absolutely motionless because they were so close at hand.

After a time, as I went on breathing, I began to sicken of the smell of my blood; it was as if it belonged to a corpse. The hot sun burned down on me remorselessly. After a while blood takes on a vile, abominable smell, it begins to break up and disintegrate with the sun and wind. I thought I was going to choke. I felt I couldn't hang on any longer. Then pain began, in my hand, and my head, and my legs. It began to hit me and paralyze me. My whole body was in pain, and I couldn't move. I lay crumpled over my unendurable wounds.

I'll speak to them, I thought. Then I thought, no I won't. But I felt I'd rather die than suffer the pain racking my whole body. I'll speak to them, I thought, and either they'll pick me up and give me treatment, or they'll shoot me and put me out of my torment.

I raised my head from the ground. My right eye was clogged with blood and dirt. It was lucky that there was some earth on the asphalt, because it had caked the wound on my head and closed it up. The flow of blood from my hand had stopped because it was pressed up under my chest, but I saw that the palm had turned black and dried out, so that it seemed no more than skin and bone.

As I looked round, I saw them sitting by the side of the

building. The tank was stationary, but some of the men were still on alert. If they see me moving my head in their direction, I thought, they'll open fire on me straightaway. I said, in a low voice: "*Khawaja.*" This was what they used to call the Jews years ago in Palestine, and it was the only word I could think of to address them. "*Khawaja,*" I said. Random firing started up in all directions. They couldn't work out where the voice was coming from, and one of them began to shout through a loud-hailer: "Terrorist! Palestinian! Give yourself up!" They were in a woefully confused state, and started firing with their tank guns towards the orchards that were on the other side of the wall behind me. "No, I'm here," I said. "I'm wounded." One of them noticed me, then they all saw me, and pointed their rifles at me. "Shut up!" they shouted, and started to hurl insults about my sister and my mother. "Shut up, you pimp! Who's with you?" "Who's with me?" I said. "Who do you think there is? There's no one with me." The man in charge of the tank's gun aimed it at me, and one of them said: "Are you armed?" "How can I be armed," I said. "Can't you see I'm wounded?"

They started talking to one another in Hebrew, then, after fifteen minutes, two of them came out of the building, with two more running behind them to cover them. They had a blanket, which they placed on the ground and rolled me on to, turning me over onto my back. I looked in front of me, and saw the white vehicle we'd been traveling in, crashed against the wall. It was black now, gutted by fire, and near it I saw two bodies. One of them I recognized as Ibrahim's. The door on his side of the car was open, and he was lying on the ground in his yellow short-sleeved pullover and military pants. The other was one of the young men, who'd jumped from the car. The rest had been burned to death in the fire which had flared up inside. I'd felt the hot air blowing over me from where I was on the ground.

The two of them carried me on the blanket, then, when they heard firing close by, they threw me on to the ground and went back into the building and opened fire, leaving me in the middle of the road. I tried to crawl, but was totally unable to move.

When the firing had died down, they ran back up to me, grasped the corners of the blanket, dragged me along the ground and dumped me near the building. At once the wound in my head opened and the blood began to well out as if from a fountain or tap, onto my face. They looked at me and some of them spat at me; then they turned and left. One of them was still standing near me, and I said: "Tie up my hand and my head." "I haven't got any bandages on me," he said. "Have you got any money?" "Search me," I said.

I expected him to take the money I had and give me treatment. I had my monthly stipend, about 900 Lebanese pounds, in my pocket.

He came up to me and went down on one knee. Then he opened my pocket, took out the cash and put it in his own pocket. He saw I also had three identity cards, looked at one of them, said, "An officer as well!" and tossed it onto my chest. "Tie up my hand," I said. "I'm not tying it up for you," he said. "Have you got any more money on you?" "Look for yourself," I said.

He came back, searched in the other pocket and took out a small notebook drenched with blood, which he looked at contemptuously and threw away. I breathed a sigh of relief, since the notebook had contained the names of some of the men who were on duty.

"Don't you have any more money?" he said.

"You've taken everything I've got," I said. "Tie up my hand."

He walked away and left me.

The pain deepened my exhaustion. The blood wouldn't stop draining away, and I felt my heart pounding violently. I urinated without feeling it, and vomited, then vomited again. Blood flowed out of my mouth, and I lost consciousness; then I came to again, sweating profusely and gripped by an intense cold. I retched, but nothing would come up. I woke to find myself in a military vehicle like a personnel transporter, and asked one of the men on it to put the blanket on my head. He trod on my head with his soldier's boot, insulted my sister and called me a pimp. "Our heads weren't made to be trampled on," I said.

There was a crashing sound in my head. Inside the transporter was like a big box containing smaller boxes of rifle shot, with seats that folded back against the sides. As it started, I tried unsuccessfully to imagine where we might be going. They put us down at a branch first aid post, where I was given an injection in my leg and a serum bag for intravenous feeding. Then we were transported in an ordinary ambulance from the first aid post to a field hospital, apparently at al-Doha. It was sunset, and there were pines and birdsong. We were taken inside, and in the ward one of them pointed to my arm and said to the other: "Cut his hand off." He took my hand and turned it over, seeing how the bullet had scraped off all the flesh and how the bone stood out exposed through the muscles.

I began to shout and curse. "Fascists! Nazis! Why do you want to cut my hand off?"

I managed to move two fingers. "Look," I said, "here's my hand moving. Why do you want to cut it off?" An old man came into the room, dressed in a military uniform with a white coat over it; he seemed to be a doctor and the others male nurses. He examined my hand and moved it about, then signaled to one of the nurses to stitch it up. Another began to stitch my head, and others worked on my feet. I'd received nine bullet wounds in all: one in the head, one in my right hand, four in my right leg, one in my left leg and two in my left hand.

(5)

While they were treating me, they gathered round and started asking questions. Some of them spoke good Arabic.

"Do you like the Jews?" one of them asked.

"That's a silly question," I said. "We've nothing against the Jews. They're our cousins."

"So why are you fighting us?"

"I'll tell you," I said. "But let me ask you a question first. Where do you come from?"

"I'm an Iraqi Jew."

"How about that fellow next to you?"

"He's Yemeni."

"And him?"

"He's from Canada."

"All right then, so you're all from different countries. Palestine's our country. And you're there occupying it against our will."

The soldier who was speaking to me carried on stitching my hand, but a fair-haired man with glasses got up and punched me in the face.

The others shook their heads, finished their work and walked away. Before they left they put me back on the stretcher and tied my whole body with cord right up to the neck.

When they came back they blindfolded me with a headcloth and carried me out. I don't know where they took me then. My throat was dry and I started to shout: "Water! Water!" My tongue felt like a file, but whenever I spoke, one of them would come up and say: "Be quiet, you pimp. There's no water." When I didn't reply, he'd grab me by the throat and grip it as hard as he could, as though he wanted to strangle me; and when I cried out he'd tell me to shut up. He'd also, with a sarcastic gesture, shake the serum being injected into my hand.

Then there were footsteps on the stairs, and I heard them speak to one another in Hebrew. "Do you speak Hebrew?" they asked me.

They lifted me up and took me out again, and I was able to sense an open space through the headcloth. Then there was a sound like that of helicopter propellers, and, together with some other wounded men, I was taken aboard and flown off.

(6)

When they took the blindfold from my eyes, I found myself in a room with two beds and two washbasins, and there was a young man dressed in civilian clothes, holding a pen and a notebook in his hand. "Welcome," he said,

119

"and may God bless you. How are you now? I hope you're feeling better."

He was an Iraqi Jew, and when I saw his pen and notebook and civilian clothes, I realized that he was an interrogator, who was in search of speedy information. He offered me some tea. "Are you all right now?" he asked. "And how are things in the Solom Quarter?" (He meant Sullam Quarter.) "What were you doing there? No, don't try and talk. Take your time. Have some tea first."

Then he began:

"Your name?" he said.

"Walid al-Alami."

"Why are you lying? We don't want lies."

I'd forgotten my operational name that was written on the three identity cards they'd taken; the cards of the joint command and the organization and the permit for carrying firearms.

During the investigation he got nothing whatever out of me.

"According to your identity card," he said, "you're a first lieutenant."

"I'm in the militia," I said.

"How did you reach the rank of first lieutenant?"

"I'm not a first lieutenant, or a second lieutenant either. It's just a question of the terms of service I insisted on. They wrote that rank on the identity card so that I could get better rations."

"What's your profession?"

"I'm a blacksmith."

"What were you trained for?"

"Only to use the Kalashnikov and hand grenades."

"And rocket propelled grenades?"

"Among the Palestinians even small boys fire RPGs."

He asked me about the ammunition depots, and I told him that the Israeli air strikes had hit the biggest and most important of them all, at the Cité Sportif (I knew for a fact that the Cité Sportif had been the provision store for rice and sugar), and I also told him that these strikes had forced the resistance to evacuate the store of arms there and distribute them to all the buildings in Beirut.

"How," he asked.

"They put five or ten crates of weapons in each building."

Then he asked me about the leaders of the resistance. Where were they, and where did they live?

"I'd like to ask you a question," I said. "Do you know where Begin and Sharon are at this moment?" He said he didn't.

"I'm in exactly the same position."

"Haven't you seen them?"

"I've seen them at rallies I've attended, but I don't know what they do or where they are."

He got out some maps.

"This is the Western Sector," he said. "Here's the Cité Sportif."

The map was actually a very clear aerial photograph. I could see the road block mounted by the Resistance in front of the Cité Sportif, and the various roads and streets, including our home. And I could see the cross-roads by the Rahmeh Building in Fakihani, and the playground, and the Sabra and Shatila camps.

"Where's this?" he asked.

"I don't know."

He indicated a spot with his finger.

"Here's Shatila camp," he said, "and there's a tunnel leading to Borj al-Barajneh, isn't there?"

"If there was a tunnel," I said, "I'm sure I would have heard about it. Whoever told you about it was lying."

(7)

After interrogation came hospital. Sometimes I'd come across wounded people I knew, but we'd pretend to be strangers, then communicate in secret. I managed to learn that we were in Tel Aviv.

I was given tranquilizers to combat the intense pain. When they wanted to re-interrogate me, they'd drag the bed along on its castors to the room set aside for questioning, but again they got nothing out of me.

There was a doctor in the interrogation room with a needle in his hand; it contained poison, he said, and he'd inject it into the intravenous drip if I didn't talk. I said I'd told them all I knew and they could do what they liked.

One of them said: "I'll bring your mother and sister in and screw them."

"Do what you like," I said. "I'm doing everything I can to help you."

Another one said: "We'll shave your mustache off",* then got up and cut half of it off.

"Do what you like," I said.

He hit me in the face and subjected me to a volley of curses.

---

* This insult and the preceding insult to the prisoner's mother and sister are direct assaults on the prisoner's sense of manly pride. Traditionally, an Arab man has special responsibility for protecting the honor of the womenfolk of his blood. The mustache is an important symbol of his manhood, and the shaving of it by an enemy constitutes a deliberate attack on this manhood.

The place was a hospital and a prison combined. There were chains on our feet, and the nurse who fed me would shove the spoon in my mouth as if she wanted to break my teeth. When the Red Cross came they took our beds and hid us in other rooms.

Twenty days later I saw a lady from the Red Cross passing in the corridor, and called out at the top of my voice: "Red Cross! Red Cross!"

She stopped at the door.

"What is it?" she asked in Classical Arabic.

"I've been here for twenty days," I said. "Whenever you come, they smuggle us out."

She produced three forms and wrote my name and address on them. Then she said that a group of prisoners was to be handed over in exchange for an Israeli pilot and the bodies of some Israelis that were being held by the Resistance. If things worked out as planned, they'd try and include some of the wounded who were now in Israel.

"Can you walk?" she asked.

"I can crawl if I have to. The main thing is to get out of here."

Next morning a committee from the Red Cross came, accompanied by the Israeli doctors. They unlocked my chains, and I got out of bed to stand up, but the room swirled round me and I fell. They picked me up, and again I tried to stand. A doctor from the Red Cross stood me by the bed and told me to sit down on the edge of it. He recorded my prison number and name, then said in English: "He's leaving."

"His wound hasn't healed yet," said the Israeli doctor.

"That's no problem," he said. "He can finish his treatment abroad."

That afternoon I slept, and saw the whole scene again in my dream, as if it were happening at that moment—how we'd been wounded, and the burnt out car. I wept, then woke.

The room had a curtain, and in it was a tiny hole through which a huge tree was visible. The sun would be reflected on to the curtain, and through it I could make out twenty-five or so birds twittering on the branches of the tree. Their shadows would be cast on the curtain, and I'd listen to their song.

I felt at peace. Release was certainly on the way, and when I left I'd see my children, I'd rejoin the Resistance, I'd be free of all the torment, all the anguished thoughts of a prisoner of war. No longer would I wish, a thousand times a day, that I'd died before they'd taken me.

(9)

On the twenty-third day they brought us blue overalls, boots, socks and underclothes and told us to get dressed. I was sure we were leaving here for prison. Some of the other patients helped me into my clothes.

About fifty of us stood in a line till the Red Cross bus arrived, when we were called out by name. In the office they gave us back our personal belongings—keeping the two bullets I'd had left and, of course, the identity cards. I put on my watch, which was marked with my own blood. It had stopped at the very moment I was hit.

The bus moved off, and I saw the land and orchards

and trees and sky of Palestine, its cotton fields and the grapes in its vineyards—our country which we're forbidden even to approach. We traveled down the highway towards Natanya, and saw Haifa, Mount Carmel, the port, the refinery and the railway line. By the sides of the road we saw abandoned Arab houses with the names of their owners still on the doors.

I wept, not alone, but with all the prisoners returning with me on the bus. I hadn't wept since I was wounded, but I wept now. There was the country that was beyond my reach, and there was the sea—the sea shimmering and gleaming behind the roofs of Shuwaika, the village which I was even now leaving behind me! It had nothing to say to us, as if it had no understanding of the secret of our tears.

We reached Tyre, where I got in touch with my relations. The day I arrived was the very day on which they'd told my wife of my death in battle; it had already been officially announced, but they'd hidden the news from her because she was a nursing mother and they were afraid of the effects on my baby daughter.

Three days later I was on the sea, in the last ship of fighters leaving Beirut. But I didn't talk with the sea.

Now I understand the secret of my tears.

About the Translators

Peter Clark was born in Sheffield, England and has two degrees in History. He has been employed by the British Council since 1967 and as British Council representative has worked in Jordan, Lebanon, Sudan, Yemen, Tunisia and, at present, in the United Arab Emirates. This long sojourn in so many countries of the Arab world has given him an intimate knowledge not only of Arabic culture as a whole, but also of the various local sub-cultures of the different Arab countries where he lived in and performed his intercultural responsibilities with so much success. Among his works is *Henry Hallam*, published in the Twayne English Series in 1982. He is also the author of a study on the novelist and translator, *Mamaduke Pickthall, British Muslim* (1986) and has translated *Karari: The Sudanese Account of the Battle of Omdurman*, by Ismat Hasan Zulfo (1980), and *Dubai Tales* by Mohammad al-Murr (1991).

Christopher Tingley was born in Brighton, England, and was educated at the universities of London and

Leeds. Following initial teaching experience in Germany and Britain, he lectured in the fields of English Language and Linguistics at the University of Constantine, Algeria, the University of Ghana, the National University of Rwanda and the University of Ouagadougou, Burkina Faso. In the field of translation, he collaborated with the author on the translation of the extracts of Arabic poetry in S. K. Jayyusi's two volume work *Trends and Movements in Modern Arabic Poetry*; for PROTA, he has co-translated (with Olive and Lorne Kenny as first translators) Yusuf al-Qaid's novel, *War in the Land of Egypt* (1986) and many short stories.